HOB
AND THE
Goblins

"Hob works when he lives in a house.
He tidies away abandoned things, like scraps
of quarrels, or pieces of spite. He banishes
small troubles, makes ghosts happy, soothes
tired curtains, charms kettles into singing,
and stops milk sulking."

Hob, the friendly house spirit, has found a
new family to take care of, but the house
they live in proves to hold more than just
"FloorShiver" and "PlasterCrack." Hob is
suddenly confronted with dwarfs, witches,
goblins, gremlins, and a dark secret that
hides the path to a crock of gold. He must
use all his tricks, cunning, and invisible
powers if he is to see the adventure through
to its hair-raising conclusion.

William Mayne's unique language conjures
up a magical world where children can
create their own imaginative visions. Norman
Messenger's spriteful Hobgoblin alphabet
adds to the mystery and power of this
spellbinding tale.

WILLIAM MAYNE
HOB
AND THE
GOBLINS

ILLUSTRATED BY

NORMAN MESSENGER

A DORLING KINDERSLEY BOOK
First American Edition, 1994
2 4 6 8 10 9 7 5 3 1
Published in the United States by
Dorling Kindersley Publishing, Inc.,
95 Madison Avenue, New York, New York 10016

Text copyright ©1993 William Mayne
Illustration copyright © 1993 Norman Messenger

CIP data is available.

ISBN 1-56458-713-4

Color reproduction by DOT Gradations Ltd.
Printed in Great Britain by Butler and Tanner

Illustrated by Norman Messenger
Designed by Ian Butterworth

ONE

ob stood in hot sunshine, on cold snow. They were all in a park in the middle of London.

"Hob is uncomfortable," he said. "It isn't the Hot or the Cold. Hob does not mind those."

People walked past quickly. Perhaps they were going to play. "Lovely day," said one. Snow crunched under their feet. The words turned to steam as they were spoken.

"Slippery underfoot," said another, waving an umbrella.

Hob thought, "I wonder where I am, and I wonder when it is." He felt somebody-else-ish.

"Sunlight is not Hob's friend," he said. "Why am I in it?"

He took off his hat to scratch his head and help him think. He wondered why he had a hat.

"Hob does not have a hat," he said. "Hob does not

have clothes unless he is given them."

He looked at himself. He was invisible and had to look hard. He was wearing only a hat. No one else saw him at all.

A puzzled dog sniffed at him, went away, and kept looking back. Hob was a smell it wanted to see.

Hob began to remember where he had been; the cat, a dog, a rabbit, a cutch under the stairs of a house full of children who had known about Hob. When they grew up they forgot. Now Hob was beginning to forget too.

"The older they got the more muddle they left. Hob would be all night seeing to things, setting them right."

Hob works when he lives in a house. He tidies away abandoned things, like scraps of quarrel, or pieces of spite. He banishes small troubles, makes ghosts happy, soothes tired curtains, charms kettles into singing, and stops milk sulking.

If he is comfortable he stays as long as possible. The people leave him presents. What he can eat, like pie or cake, is very good; what he can smoke in his pipe is excellent. One thing he must not be given; but, sooner or later, people hope to please, forget the rule, and leave out a set of clothes.

Hob has to put them on. They turn him vain and proud; he thinks how fine he looks, and leaves at once, pleased to be well dressed. He must wear them until they wear out.

He does good deeds no more. He lets Mischief into

the house, and does not care, Rot climbs the roof and he madly disregards it, Worry goes down the chimney and he yawns.

"Hat wears me with style," said Hob, looking at it. It was a good hat with a brim turned up all round. "We look smart."

He remembered buttons with weskit. The buttons had departed one by one. There had been laces full of shoe, holes full of sock. The laces had become wildly undone, tripped Hob up and escaped with the shoes and the socks.

He had had pockets with breeches, a row of neat little holes with a belt round them and a buckle to keep them together. The breeches had vanished when the holes in the belt ganged up and stopped working.

There had been a memory knot and a handkerchee to keep it in. The knot untied and the handkerchee blew away.

Toggles had taken care of a coat until it was stolen by an old troll from the Swedish embassy.

"Now I am homesick for a new home, a new cutch underneath the stairs, a new family to look after. It is my duty."

Only the hat kept Hob out of the houses, and at the same time longing for a family. Its duty was to sit quietly on his head, not very clever, but in charge, made of gray felt. Paper hats have more to say, sometimes with a picture of the Queen.

"Perhaps only one of us is in fashion now," said Hob.

Hob walked to the park gates. If humans could see his footprints on the soft snow they would not have known whose they were. No one has caught Hob and measured his feet.

Hob did not understand what he saw outside the gates. "People sitting in cupboards with glass doors," he said. "The cupboards roaring about." Cars had not begun when he left the last house. "The horses must be inside," he thought.

He did not remember bicycles either. The spokes of the wheels twinkled like a new headache, so he did not watch.

Humans cannot see Hob unless he wishes them to. Passersby were walking through him. He stood in a line of people who were not moving. Hob wondered why they tramped and tramped in the cold snow in the same place, working hard but going nowhere – not very far.

A noisy red house was suddenly beside him. The people went into it one by one and sat down in the chairs.

"Mind the doors," said someone who lived in the red house already. "All aboard."

"Hob has been invited," said Hob. "I may go in."

He climbed up the big steps to the high floor and the doors swung closed behind him.

Hob went straight for the staircase, all among the feet of people, and up to see the bedrooms. There were narrow beds, with people sitting on them, looking out of the windows.

"What a lot live here," said Hob. "Hob will stay quiet downstairs until I know them better."

Hob did not like the way scenery was being dragged under the house in a lumpy way. They should both keep still.

People stood up, and one of them rang a bell.

"Calling for the maid," said Hob. But there were no maids. People left without saying good-bye. Luckily, thought Hob, scenery stopped and waited for them.

Under the stairs there were cupboards. "They are expecting me," said Hob, opening one little door and then another. "Excuse Hob. He does not mean to intrude," he said each time. But no one lived there, he decided.

"Not this, it is too small," said Hob, looking in one. "And this is full of strings. This one is locked. This is full of ham sandwiches, but Hob only eats what he is given. But this cupboard will make a cutch." He went from one to another until he found one where he could stretch out and sleep.

"But where's the fireplace?" he said. "A home without a hearth is of little worth." He knows these things.

But it was far into day and he was tired. He climbed in, perched the good gray hat on his tummy, and went to sleep.

Lumpy scenery still hurried under the house. "Hob cannot see it," said Hob. "But he feels it under him."

A long time later he woke. The house was quiet and still.

"They are all asleep," said Hob. "They will not see Hob."

He came out of the cutch. Strange stars hung in the sky in straight lines. Next door there was a house like the one he was in, and another beyond, and more and more.

"The house has got its street back," thought Hob, because that was how the row seemed to him.

There were no people in the house now, only their mess and muddle. The floors were littered with scraps of paper, and the windows were grimy. Hob found the poker sticking into the floor, and the tongs fixed down.

"A house cannot be empty," said Hob. "If someone lives in it Hob should be able to tell. There must be something here."

No one had left him anything to eat.

"Hob with a hat is not Hob," he said at last. "I cannot see what mischiefs are about while I have clothes."

He sat in a chair facing a window. It should have been facing a fireplace, because the poker was on one side and the tongs on the other. He did not know that he was in the driver's seat of a red London bus, and that the poker and the tongs were the gear stick and the brake. He thought the steering wheel was there to help him climb into the chair.

"Hob has gone backward," he thought. "I have come to the time before fires and hearths. This red house is a cave."

When the stars faded and daylight came, he climbed into his new cutch and waited to see what was to happen today, tomorrow, or yesterday.

"It is not quite home," he said. "Hob still has the hat."

If you have a hat you cannot get rid of, it is best to keep it happy. An unhappy hat will give you a headache or rub your ears. At the very least it will eat your hair and make you bald. He carefully hung it on a hook outside his cutch, closed the door, and shut his eyes.

ob had not been asleep long before scenery began moving again. Houses outside were not alarmed. Some were having sleep washed from windows. Others smoked thoughtfully. One of them had shyly put on ivy trousers. Many had made friends with birds and wore nests in their ears.

Sometimes everything stood still, the red house's door would open, and people come in.

Hob sat in his cutch with the door open. He filled his pipe and lit it. He smoked, puff, puff. It helped him think.

People began to shout. He did not know why. They shouted, "Fire, fire," and waved their arms.

"I'm glad they want a fire," said Hob. "No house is complete without one. The hearth is the heart." He blew a large smoke ring that wandered about smiling.

The man sitting between the poker and tongs tried to pull them from the floor. People fell down.

The man pulled a red thing from the wall, told everyone to sit down, and marched up the middle of the bus.

"The teapot," thought Hob. "I'm longing for a cup."

The man was the driver. He banged the red thing on the floor under the stairs, and pointed it at Hob, in his cutch.

"Hob is first," thought Hob. He was right, but he did not get tea. He was sprayed with a white powder that stuck to him, and he was visible. The passengers saw him for a moment and shrieked. Hob sneezed. His pipe went straight out.

"It looks like a ghost or monster," said a passenger.

"It was just smoke," said the driver.

"Well done, Charlie Grimes," said an old lady from the same street. "You have saved us from being burned up."

"It's nothing," said Charlie. "I've extinguished it." He peered into the cutch, but Hob could not be seen.

"You put Hob's pipe out," said Hob. "My tobacco is ruined."

"There is something wrong," said Charlie. "I must go back to the depot. You'll have to get off at the next stop."

They all did, except for Charlie the driver, and the old lady.

"You go straight past my road on the way to the depot," said the old lady. "You drive and I'll watch for smoke."

Hob cleaned his pipe out. "It has been spoiled

again," he said. Once the children of a house blew bubbles with it and filled it with soapy water.

"Hob's not himself yet," he said. "I'm still owned by a hat. I wish someone would take it away." He sat and scraped, scenery went by, and no one got on or off.

"This bus has problems," Charlie told the old lady. "One week it had five flat tires, and the lamps wouldn't work. You turned them on, and nothing came along the wires. Nothing."

"There," said Hob. "Hob hopes this pipe will work again."

"And once," said Charlie, "she got jammed against the top of the tunnel. She got frightened and had to be pulled out backward. It wasn't my fault: the old girl has been through hundreds of time. Now if anything at all goes wrong I go straight to the depot."

"Quite right, Mr. Grimes," said the old lady.

"These things are not natural," said Hob. "If the house gets flat-tired it's because it has been working too hard. It gets stuck in holes because it isn't a rabbit. Or perhaps there is a problem visitor. I can't tell with this hat on."

Something chuckled in a cruel way not far off. It might have been in the bus, or in scenery lumbering past.

"There is the problem," said Hob. "But I still have a hat."

The chuckle came again.

"And there are funny noises," said Charlie. "Did

you hear that? It's something wanting to go wrong."

"It's just getting old, Charlie," said the old lady.

Hob said, "Could be a Gremlin. The hat won't let me see it."

"I'll drop you off at your house," said Charlie, "go home for a cup of tea with my ham sandwiches, and then go to the depot."

Near the stairs the Gremlin laughed under its breath. "Now is my chance," it said, in a gritty voice.

"Hob would know what to do if he was himself," said Hob.

The bus stopped in the side road. "Thank you," said the old lady. "My regards to Mrs. Grimes and children, and the bird."

Charlie pulled the door lever, said Good-bye, and closed the door. "They'll never know I took a short-cut," he said.

"Ha," said the Gremlin.

Hob longed to deal with the Gremlin. He knew he was an expert, if it wasn't for that hat. Charlie double-parked outside his own house, sounded the horn and rang the bell, opened the doors and let himself out.

The Gremlin laughed aloud.

"Hob wishes he could see you," said Hob. He heard the Gremlin walking among the seats.

It fancied Hob's hat hanging by Hob's cutch. It took it, put it on and pulled it down tight. It climbed into the driving seat. It began to pull and push at the lever that opened and closed the doors. It closed them, then opened them suddenly. Charlie was halfway up the garden path, but turned to see what was going on, wondering why his bus was hissing at him. Hob thought he should hurry after him and tell him about the Gremlin.

But the doors closed when Hob was on the top step. When they opened again he was down on the next one. When they closed for the last time they pushed him out between the parked cars.

Charlie gave a yell, put his foot through Hob, and tried to press the emergency door button. But the Gremlin had started the engine and begun to drive away.

"Come back," shouted Charlie, running after it. The Gremlin got into the middle of the road, put his foot down, and hurtled between the parked cars in a cloud of diesel smoke.

"There's a Gremlin," said Hob. "Didn't you know?"

"I always took my lucky rabbit's foot," said Charlie. He realized he was speaking to no one. "But you spoke to me," he said. "What are you?"

Hob was too happy to explain. "Hob is free," he said.

"Only if you hold a pensioner's card," said Charlie. "Come out of hiding, whoever you are, and show it to me."

"The Gremlin took my hat," said Hob. "I can work again."

Alice Grimes came out of the house. "I knew it was you," she said to Charlie. "The one daft enough to bring a bus down our road. Where do you think you are? Piccadilly Circus?"

"I don't know," said Charlie. "First the bus sets itself on fire, then it gets stolen, then I hear strange voices telling me it's free, and now you're cross. I only wanted a cup of tea with my ham sandwiches, and they're still in the bus."

"The bus has gone off toward Waterloo Station," said Alice.

"I'll telephone," said Charlie. "I don't know what to say."

Hob sat under a tree, smoked his pipe, and had a little nap.

He woke up when the gate clicked open and then shut. Two men came along the path and tapped at the door.

"Oh, it's you," said Charlie. "Are you coming in?"

"We'll say what we have to out here, Charlie Grimes," said one of the men, an inspector from the depot. "You have broken several company rules. You let the bus catch fire, and turned all the passengers off. You bring it along a road it should only see the ends of, and you let someone steal it. Mr. Grimes, the company feels you would be better off doing a simpler job somewhere else."

"But I can explain," said Charlie. "It was a Gremlin."

"We don't care who it was," said the Inspector. "Do we? That bus ended in the River Thames. There was a gray hat floated away, and that was all. Buses cost money, you know."

Charlie went into the house without shutting the door.

"That's so like a Gremlin," said Hob, blowing a smoke ring full of words inside a bubble.

The bubble burst over the men at the gate, and the words came out. "Gremlins indeed!" said one to the other.

Hob got up and walked to the door. He tapped on it.

"Come in and shut the door," said Alice. "Men and children are all the same." But when she looked no one was there.

"Hob has been invited in," said Hob. "He's found somewhere to live. There'll be plenty to do. How many children are there? And what bird have they got? Not too big, I hope."

Mrs. Grimes closed the door firmly. "Now Charlie," she said. "What are we going to do?"

"Move to the country," said Charlie. "Lock, stock, and barrel. We can do it. We actually can."

"Three children," thought Hob. "What strange names."

"Oh Charlie," said Alice. "I've always wanted to live in a cottage among green fields with an apple tree and a goat."

THREE

ob was looking
about at where he was going to live. "She said Come
in," he said. "I will if it feels right."

A voice said, "Nup, nup, skwee." Hob knew it
meant, "Look out, something has crept in."

"Hob was invited," said Hob, seeing Budgie.

"Who's a pretty boy, then?" said Budgie.

"A blue sparrow," Hob thought. "It'll talk all night."

Alice Grimes said, "Look, Charlie, even Budgie is
excited."

Hob made faces until Budgie scattered seed out of
the cage, washed her face in the drinking water and
sneezed.

"We'll have an aviary," said Charlie. "A flock of
budgies."

"We'll solve that when we come to it," said Hob,
not liking the idea. "Now, what's moving about in here?"

A cradle was swinging from side to side. Baby was

singing to itself. Hob climbed up to see what kind of animal it was.

"A human," he decided, when it smiled at him. "It has no hair, a smile with no teeth, and it dribbles. Is it very new or very old? Hob must find out. Old ones know too much, and young ones too little."

He set the cradle swinging and went to try the stairs. Hob's home is a cutch under the stairs.

Charlie came rushing up to change from bus-driver uniform. Bedclothes slept on the bed, and pictures on the walls saw themselves in dressing-table mirrors. Empty nighty faced lonely day in a girl's room, and a boy's neglected hairbrush wondered why it was never used.

In the bathroom, toothbrush was miserable too. "Babies and grandfathers have no teeth," said Hob.

Downstairs, Charlie in his best clothes, and Alice powdering her nose, were getting ready to go out.

"Why does she dab flour on herself?" said Hob. "Are they baking her?"

"Hurry," said Charlie. "He might have sold it."

"Nobody wants to buy a ruin in the middle of nowhere," said Alice, putting away the powder puff.

"It's been empty," said Charlie, "since Great-Uncle Fluellen vanished a hundred years ago. It's ours still if the lawyer hasn't sold it. I'm tired of living in town, so I hope he hasn't."

Alice popped the baby in the pram. Hob saw it smile at her. "Hob wonders whether it means it," said Hob. "You can't tell."

But actually, mothers can. She patted Baby on the back, and it said "Borp" in a charming way.

"Very cunning," said Hob, "old or new."

He was alone in the house, with a clock ticking, and Budgie snapping her beak. Hob opened the cupboard under the stairs cautiously. "No one knows who's here first," he said looking at the top step from underneath. "Hob's eye view," he said. "But can Hob stretch out?"

He could, in the secret space under the landing floor. "Hob's cutch," he said, "ready-made for me. I'll go to sleep."

He found a rug to lie on, in a pram with a wooden doll in it.

"That belongs to Meg," sang Budgie. "I'll tell."

Hob found himself a cover to lie under.

"That's the best tray-cloth," sang Budgie.

"Hob hasn't slept in a bed in a hundred years," said Hob. He made his bed and went to sleep. He woke up to the noise of children running upstairs and thumping across the landing.

"The house is falling in," he thought, banging his head on the floor above him, and his heels on the ceiling below. "Hob expects one of each kind, not fifty." He rubbed his head and his heels, and went to sleep again.

Later he woke to a quiet house. He crept out of the cutch and walked up the stairs on their proper side. At the top he looked around.

A boy called Tom was dreaming adventure on the

moon. "Strange clothes they wear there," said Hob.
"Hob hopes he does not bring back a Moonling, so
difficult to get rid of."

A girl called Meg was dreaming of a blue pony
with long mane and tail, running, running, across the
fields.

Baby in the cot upstairs was dreaming magic.

"That settles it," said Hob. "It's a young one. Hob
will have to be careful, or it will dream him."

Alice was dreaming of a lovely cottage with flowers
tall against the front, pretty thatch, and skies all blue.

Next to her Charlie was half awake, wondering
whether he had done the right things all day. In the
end he went downstairs to make a cup of tea. "No
good watching the dark," he said. Hob went down
too. Hob likes a cup of tea.

Charlie dropped a cup and saucer. Hob caught the
cup, but the saucer broke on the floor. Alice woke
and came down.

"I couldn't sleep either," she said. "Let's set the fire
going and sit beside it and drink our tea."

Hob went to look at the fire. Under its ash, Fire
was eating coal, hiccuping sparks, smoke coming
from his head.

"Nothing has changed," said Hob. "Bring three cups."

Alice and Charlie came through, wondering why
there were three cups on the tray, and where the
tray-cloth was.

"Hob has borrowed it," said Budgie sneakily. No
one heard.

"I've poured three cups after all," said Alice, later.

"One for luck," said Charlie.

"We have been lucky," said Alice. "Getting there just in time to stop the lawyer selling the cottage. It's going to be so nice."

"You've never seen it," said Charlie. "I saw it when I was little, but I have forgotten it."

"It will be an adventure," said Alice. "We can keep hens."

They sat and talked and had two cups of tea each.

Hob helped himself to more sugar.

"I'll hire a van," said Charlie. "We can go when we want."

"If you can find the way," said Alice. "It isn't on the map."

"We'll ask when we get near," said Charlie. "Now that's settled, let's get some sleep."

Off they went, and Hob sat beside the fire dipping his finger in the sugar basin and listening for problems in the house.

"Not every address is perfect," he said to Budgie. "Where are they going? Hob was asleep and did not hear."

Budgie could not say the words, and thought she did not know them. Hob climbed into his cutch at daybreak.

There was a photograph of·the cottage the next night, with its name written on it. The cottage was neat but dark, with big stones in the garden and in the fields behind. Hob did not understand words written down, and Budgie could not read. No one else said the name. They just called it "The Cottage."

"It won't be anywhere dreadful," said Hob. "Why worry?"

A week went by. Hob had to deal with Hole, who came in on a shoe and began to nest in a carpet. Hole went to live in a road with workmen to feed him and lamps round him at night.

"It's more fun than carpets," he said. "Thank you, Hob."

Charlie brought boxes for Alice to fill with household things. "Put Budgie in the bottom," said Hob, and she flew into a rage.

One morning Charlie went out early and came back with a big van. He began to fill it with the boxes. Then came the furniture, the carpets, the gardening things, and the clothes.

"Shall I go or stay?" said Hob. "I wish I knew where they are going. Humans do take a lot of things about."

"Don't forget Budgie," said Alice.

"Don't forget the sandwiches," said Tom.

"Forget Hob," said Hob. "Hob does not feel like another change. There's no need for me to flit. I'll just see them off."

"Don't forget Baby," called Meg.

"Good-bye, Charlie," said the old lady from down the road. "You haven't told me your new address."

"I might visit them," said Hob. "If it's not far."

"It is a romantic name," said Alice.

"It's a bit fancy," said Charlie.

"Fairy Ring Cottage," said Meg. "Isn't that nice?"

"Fairy Ring Cottage!" said Hob, horrified, hardly
able to believe what he heard. His bristly hair stood
up like wire. He felt it squirm. "The wickedest house
in the country, the worst luck in the world. I must tell
them not to go."

"Fairy Ring Cottage," said the old lady. "How
sweet."

Charlie started the engine and they were moving.

Hob ran through the old lady, through the gate,
and after the van. When it slowed at the corner
before turning left, Hob took hold of the back and
fell down inside among the belongings. "These inno-
cent people are alone," he said, "and no one else can
help them."

FOUR

"It was a whirlwind," said the old lady, seeing Hob moving fast, invisible like air. She poured tea with two lumps because of it.

"Hob should be in his cutch," Hob said. "Not head-down doing acrobatics between pieces of furniture."

Alice reached back. "Something is rattling." She took hold of Hob's left foot and shook him until he rattled no more.

"Hob wishes he could not remember he was driving to danger," said Hob. "But he knows he will."

He burrowed under the sideboard. He found a box to sit on, and scraps of carpet for his feet. "Three cutches in a week. Hob is no traveling man. He likes one cutch forever."

When Hob is setting a house right he meets friends. They share ideas, and exchange hints on new mischief.

They also talk about dangerous places. Hob never

really forgets, but he does not always remember. Now he remembered what he had forgotten about Fairy Ring Cottage.

Fairy Ring Cottage stood over the crock of gold. It has always been known that the crock is somewhere. For a long time it had not mattered. One or two foolish men, or women, or children, had ventured through after seeing dancing inside the ring. They were still inside enjoying their very first meal, which would last forever. That is a normal danger, and nothing to be gloomy about. Just stay out of fairy rings.

A hundred years ago a sorcerer had worked out how to get the crock. His plan had been to enter the kingdom and then allow nothing to pass his lips. If he took no food, drew no breath, and spoke no word, he would be able to take the gold and come safely out again. He had taken his fiddle so that the fairies would dance and he could get away before they knew what he was after. But he did not know two important things.

First, he would be followed back into this world.

Hob sat in his bouncy cutch trying not to think of the second thing, and what might happen to his new family. He could lose them before he knew anything about them.

"Hob is not strong enough," he muttered. "Hob will not be Hob much longer." He looked miserably at the floor while he remembered the rest. He groaned.

"Something is loose," said Charlie Grimes.

"It's the bird," said Alice. "Swinging about."

It was Hob, trying not to think of dangers ahead. "If Hob," he thought, "could make them turn back, he would. If Hob could give the van an attack of Flat Tired or Dark Lamps he would. But Hob cannot do Gremlinish things."

"Picnic time," said Alice. "Sandwiches under the sideboard."

Tom's hand and arm reached in to take the box Hob sat on.

"It is heavy," said Tom. "Are they stone sandwiches?"

"Hard-boiled egg," said Alice.

Tom pulled out the box with Hob still on it. Hob jumped off, thinking about goblins, forgetting to be invisible.

"What's the matter, Tom?" said Alice. "Come on."

"Nothing," said Tom. It was difficult to explain that he had seen a little person, with a very worried look, jump off the box and scurry back under the sideboard.

When he had eaten a sandwich he told Meg about it.

"I've heard about such things," said Meg, "Perhaps it is just HitchHiker. Did you see his thumbs?"

"I saw his face," said Tom. "He wasn't happy."

"We must make him happy," said Meg. "He must have something to sit on. He can't see out of the window."

Hob was invisible now. "We won't do you any harm," said Meg. She put down a cushion for him.

"You children are playing a strange game," said Alice. "That cushion should be on the settee."

"He wants to sit under the sideboard," said Meg.

"Now you are being silly," said Charlie. "We have a long way to go and you must remain sensible."

Meg had been watching the cushion. She did not see Hob, but she saw something sit on the cushion, and she knew that someone had said "Thank you," someone of the fairy kind.

"No more imaginary friends," said Alice. "You both grew out of such nonsense long since. Understand?"

Meg and Tom nodded their heads. The more you say an imaginary friend is there, the less you are believed.

The journey began again. Baby began to cry. It was not getting its proper nap, and Baby felt sick.

"Hob can do this," said Hob. He went to sit with Baby.

"Hush, my love," said Alice, putting her hand behind her to take Baby's hand or rub its cheek. She looked round suddenly, and crossly too. "No silly tricks," she said to Tom.

Alice had taken Hob's leathery hand, and then rubbed Hob's bristly cheek. It did not feel like Baby at all.

Alice found the real hand and the proper cheek. But it was Hob who sleepified Baby with a lullaby for mice. Baby dreamed very well, a long tail and fur and two bright eyes.

Hob had to think about the sorcerer's second

mistake. Fairies will plague you, not much worse than big flies, not even having a sting. The sorcerer thought that he would be dealing only with them. He would not be, he had not been. He was meddling with a different set of creatures.

"They say fairy, but they mean something else," said Hob.

Yes, Fairy Ring Cottage stood inside a ring. Not a quaint ring of tiny toadstools, made by present-day fairies, but one built by other creatures long ago.

The ring was of stones. The cottage stood among them. They had been placed there by goblins, over a door to their wild kingdom. Men could step through among goblins, goblins could step through into the world of men.

Goblins are just as fond of their crock of gold. They have swords, and like a fight. Hob's friends had heard the rumor. The sorcerer would be out soon. The signs were clear.

"They will take over," thought Hob. "It will be me first, and then this family, living on top of the doorway. Saving this family is all Hob can do. He cannot save himself." He rocked to and fro. "It is the hardest family to save, because Charlie's great-uncle is the sorcerer. They do not deserve that sort of problem."

He brooded sadly. "It is not fair," he said, "that I should be the one to sort the matter out. Why not a boggart or a sturdy dwarf? They enjoy a fight. I am a housekeeper and keep things out of houses. I shall never be able to manage."

He forgot to stay invisible, or perhaps he fell asleep. Meg saw him sitting by Baby, and Baby smiling in dream, a harvest mouse swaying on wheat stems on a sunny day.

"Look," said Meg.

"That's him," said Tom.

"He has a nice face," said Meg.

"Stop teasing your father," said Alice.

"Ah," said Baby, asleep as a dormouse in winter.

Charlie stopped at a crossroads and looked at the map. "We'll have to ask the way," he said. "Someone will know."

The first person shook his head. "I shan't tell you the way," he said. "You'd be better off going back to London."

"Thank you," said Charlie, winding up his window. "The people here don't seem to like us."

"It was just advice," said Alice.

"Good advice," said Hob. "Take it."

"Do not go on," said a farmer's wife. "It is a wicked story about Fluellen, and foolish he was, never been seen again. You will be there in four minutes, and back after five if you have sense. What he brings out will end all our good times."

"What can he bring?" asked Charlie. "Gone a century?"

"He will bring back the crock of gold," said the woman. "And who will be coming after to fetch it back? Tell me that."

"Hob is helpless," said Hob. "Humans hear me too late."

Four minutes later the van drove into the sunset. Standing against it was a ring of stones, and standing against one of the stones, half inside the circle, was a black and white house.

"It looks lonely," said Alice. "We shall be company for it."

"Worse company is coming," said Hob. "No one hears Hob."

FIVE

ob sat under the
sideboard again, safer in some sort of cutch. The
Grimes family got out of the van, except for Baby,
who was asleep. Charlie took the cottage key from
his pocket.

"It is the key to the goblin kingdom too," said Hob.
"Hob will not go in." But he would have to if his family did.

A path wandered from the gate to the cottage,
overgrown with prickly weeds. Charlie followed it to
the house.

He looked for a keyhole, but could not find one.

"Get the door open," said Alice. "It is cold standing
here."

Charlie looked round. He was surrounded by tall
figures. The tall figures were standing stones, menac-
ing in the twilight.

"Don't be stupid, Grimes," he said to himself.

"That's what Hob thinks too," said Hob. "Come away."

Charlie was trying to find a keyhole in the side of a square-shouldered stone built like a door in the wall of the cottage.

"It'll be round the side," said Alice.

"Hob should have hidden the door," said Hob. "I did not think of it in time."

It was too late now. He heard the turning of the key. He heard the creaking of hinges. He heard the bottom of the door scrape the floor. Hob cowered with his head in his hands.

"Perhaps it is not my family any more," he said.

Baby made a noise like a jellyfish being turned out of a mold.

"Hob is taking care of the baby, so it is still his family," he decided. "What if they don't come out? What shall I do with a human baby? How would I stop it growing larger?"

Hob can grow larger in an emergency. Once a HugSnake had curled round him lovingly, hissed and hissed, and started the hug. Hob had expanded until the snake disconnected all the way down its back, snap, snap, snap, snap, and dropped to the ground in bits. It had spent the rest of the summer hugging itself together again, click by click.

Hob began to notice how sweetly Baby was sleeping, and how calm it was outside. Perhaps his worries had come with him, because there were few here.

"Beetles in the walls, a patch of Greed in a front

room, bedroom floor wants its nails trimmed, chimney is asleep, and so on. Nothing unusual. Perhaps it was all in my mind."

By torchlight, the Grimes family looked inside.

"There is no tap," said Alice, beside the old sink.

"The cottage has been empty a hundred years," said Charlie. "It will have to be modernized."

"The stairs are shaking," said Tom, climbing up a little way.

"Careful," said Alice. "You don't want them on top of you."

Hob listened. "There is a slight attack of TreadWorm. Should Hob be afraid? Perhaps Fluellen has sat down to eat and will be with the goblins forever, and Hob will only meet him the day after forever has stopped."

He looked at Baby, asleep still, not bothering to dream. He climbed over the cradle and put one bare toe on the ground.

It felt firm. "Hob walks carefully," he reminded it. "Not all solid ground is solid for me. Not all walls are real. What holds a human might not hold Hob."

He stood in the gateway of the garden. "There is no Gremlin in the van," he said. "Baby is fast asleep. But there is a strangeness I do not care for, and Hob will look."

The strangeness was in a standing stone, a distant and slow noise, coming from the root of the stone. Humans could not hear it, but it was plain to Hob.

"It is like a singing tooth, not aching yet," he said

to himself. "Perhaps it will feel pain when winter is on it. Hob will remember." He tucked the thought away, exactly.

Hob laid his hands on the next stone and felt for movement. There was none. "Fluellen is in the goblin world," he said. "Somewhere here is the door, here since the beginning, and no human has come out yet, nor goblins in my time."

Hob's time is very long, but it is all one to him. He walked to the third stone, set in the house wall like a door.

"Hob wonders," he said to it. "I do indeed." But this stone had little to say. "I think it is closed," said Hob.

He came to the cottage door. He hesitated. "Is Hob invited in, I wonder," he said. "Does he need to be?"

He saw Charlie pouring the torchlight in pools on walls and floor, the rest of the family looking from one to another.

"A box of candles," said Alice. "Every house has more candles than it ever uses. Light them, Charlie, and the fire."

Hob put his foot across the threshold. This was his family, and he followed them when they moved house. "I have flitted with them," he said. "I should come in to deal with troubles."

He went out again and gathered twigs and wood broken from trees. He brought them in and laid them beside the hearth. No one saw him. "It's a long time since fire stood here. Wake up, grate."

The grate opened its throat and yawned. It shook ash from itself, and was ready for work. Hob made a twiggy tent, and then put larger wood on.

"Feels good," said the grate. "What next? I've forgotten. The kettle boils over quite often. Is that it?"

"Fire next," said Hob. He pulled a HobLight from the pouch where he kept his pipe and tobacco. He laid the HobLight to the tent of twigs, and the flame put out a hand and laid hold of the little stems. It somersaulted, did a forward roll, and grasped the next twig and the next, until they were all burning. Then it set to work on the bigger wood, laughing and snapping its teeth, now and then sending out a spark of joy.

"Oh, oh," cried the grate. "I've missed fire for nearly a hundred years, the lovely, lovely pain."

High in the chimney jackdaws climbed out into the open air, scolding and chattering. Smoke wandered out of the chimney pot, asking who it was and where to go.

Charlie thought Alice had lit the fire, and Alice knew Charlie had. "That's very like home," she said.

Charlie went for Baby. He put the cot near the fire. Alice went for the sweeping brush and swept the kitchen floor.

Tom found a coalhouse and brought coal in. The fire sipped carefully, and brightened up. "A delicious vintage," it said. "Definitely tarry." Charlie brought in a table and four chairs.

"There's me," said Hob. "Hob's here." Charlie

scratched his head, said, "I can't add up," and went for another chair. Hob sat in it, watching and listening, alert for trouble.

There were only the ailments that old houses have, like FloorShiver, PlasterCrack, and LarderMold. There was much too little of them.

"Uncanny," said Hob. Something had driven out things like Helter scuttling under the floor, and Skelter, jumping in the loft at two in the morning, not there when you look.

Charlie was looking for a tap to fill a kettle from. Hob went to help. "A simple case of no water," he said, and went outside to search. There must be water nearby. Unless there was a lair of wild Thirsts nearby.

Charlie found water outside the back door, in a well with a low wall round it. Hob smelled water down below. He heard again the distant sound from far away, nearer, louder and clearer. "Men," he said, "put water at the top of an upside-down tower built in the ground. It can't get up to the bottom of the tower, so it feels neglected."

Charlie shone the torch down the well. "It's running clean and fresh down below," he called. He dropped a pebble in. The splash echoed up the well. The echo died away, and there was strange silence.

"Something did not like that," said Hob to himself.

Charlie did not heed the sudden silence. He lowered a bucket on a rope, and pulled it up.

Alice filled the kettle and set it on the fire. "It's like being a child again," she said, "how it was at home, no electricity, no hot water, but happy times."

"Hob hopes so," said Hob. "Indeed I do."

Alice warmed soup. Charlie took beds and sleeping bags upstairs. Hob went up under the treads, searching. He tapped nails. TreadWorm thought about things.

Hob found a cutch behind the top step, under the floor. "It may not be for long," he said.

The Grimes family went to bed. Baby did not have a bath. Teeth were brushed at the sink among the soup plates.

"We are camping," said Tom. "But tents do not have stairs."

"Sleep well," said Hob, hoping it would be so.

S I X

ob spoke to Spideree, who had stopped spinning for the year.

"What feeling does Hob get from touching the tall stones?" asked Hob. "Is it in the strands of your webs?"

"Never let it into your thoughts," said Spideree. "I don't."

"Which door did Fluellen use?" asked Hob. "To go to the goblin country?" He thought he might block it up forever.

"Hob must find these things out for himself," said Spideree, rolling up her web like a blind, and sleeping in it suddenly.

The patch of Greed was lying in a front room. "Whose are you?" asked Hob. "Greed belongs to people, not to places."

"I'm waiting for a mouth to open," said Greed. "I'll be in."

"Why didn't Fluellen take you?" asked Hob.

"He didn't want a meal where he was going," said Greed.

"Which way did he go?" asked Hob.

Greed shrugged his shoulders. "I'm food Greed," he said. "I'm waiting for my Fluellen. He'll be back for supper."

When Hob's night was over he smoked a quiet pipe beside a tired fire. As dawn crept across the land he climbed into his cutch, snuggling down into an empty mouse nest.

He did not sleep well. When all else was silent he heard the thrill of sound from far below. Sometimes there would be a sound like a long-drawn-out bang, distant and hushed.

At waking-up time Charlie and Tom began carrying in furniture from the van. Baby was having a shriek. Meg and Alice thought about curtains and rugs. It was the sort of noise that Hob could sleep through, and he slept better then.

The kitchen was looking like home, with table and chairs, the pots on a dresser, pans on a rack, and the knob of the oven polished by Meg until the fire could wink back at itself.

It was blazing refreshed after a hundred years' holiday. The house began to feel warm, though a north wind brought flakes of snow and sprinkled the roof with white.

"When we've finished we'll go shopping," said Charlie. "We'll buy enough for the winter. If we're snowed in we shan't care."

"No school," said Tom.

"Building snowmen," said Meg, catching a snowflake.

When the van was empty the family went off in it. Hob was alone again. He came out of his cutch in the dusk, put coal in the grate, sat in the hearth, and had a sleep. But all the time, like a bad dream, awake or asleep, he knew this house was the wrong place for any of them to be.

The door opened and Alice came in. "The fire is still alight," she said. "Bigger than when we went out. How can that be?"

"Someone is looking after us," said Meg. "I've seen it."

"Don't talk creepy nonsense to your mother," said Charlie. "It makes her nervous."

"But it's a kind thing," said Tom. "I saw it first."

"Well, I don't see anything," said Alice.

"Of course not," said Charlie. "Bring in some more things."

The dresser was covered with groceries, the kettle went on the fire, and the table was laid for tea.

"It's just a home," said Hob. "With its problems."

Meg handed down a scone to Hob, a shadow beside the tongs and poker. He took it carefully from her hand.

There was a creaking outside, a leathery sound.

"Hob did nothing," thought Hob. "The thing has come." When he tried to eat the scone his mouth was dry.

Something thumped the ground three times.
Something knocked on the door four or five times.
The noise was loud.

Budgie said prayers.

"If it is the end of the world," said Hob, "do not
answer."

"A visitor," said Alice. "How nice and friendly."

Hob was thinking so hard that he made himself visible. But he was down beside the fire and all the
Grimes family, except Baby, looking toward the door.

The door catch rattled. Charlie and Alice looked at
one another, not happy to have the door opened by
strangers.

"Not human, that," said Hob. No one heard him.

"We're in the country now," said Alice.
"Neighborly."

"Come in," called Charlie, getting up to meet the
visitor.

"If it's Fluellen," said Hob, "I'm not ready yet."

"I saw a light," said a voice outside. A hand
clicked the latch and a swirl of snow walked in and
made the candles flicker. It was followed by a well-
wrapped-up person, dressed in black. It stamped its
feet again.

"It's pretending," Hob said to himself. "There's
nothing inside. The clothes are empty. The door
didn't really open."

Alice saw a dear little old lady putting back the
hood of her coat and shaking snow from her boots.
"I am Mrs. Idris Evans, neighbor up the road. I came

to welcome you."

"That's very kind," said Alice.

"Long time since this room was warm," said Mrs. Evans.

"Would you like a cup of tea?" said Alice.

"No thank you," said Mrs. Evans. "You can't be too careful in this house. My mother was in service here, and had tales to tell. You know them, of course."

"No," said Charlie, wondering what he had forgotten.

"I don't want to be seen," thought Hob. "If necessary I shall get in with Baby. It'll be out of the frying pan and into the fire, because babies are not yet human."

Mrs. Evans looked at the family round the table. "How very strange," she said. "What use is a baby?"

"I quite like them," said Alice. "You know."

"You must be the mother, of course," said the visitor. "It's odd for you to bring it here. I don't think you should bring children into this house with all its dangers."

"Dangers?" said Alice.

"It's rough and ready," said Charlie. "And with not being lived in for a long time, it will take a lot of putting right."

"More than you think," said the visitor.

"We feel quite safe," said Tom. Even Baby laughed. Only Hob felt a shudder running across his shoulders.

"We don't know any stories," said Charlie. "This house belongs to us, so we have moved in."

"You should never have bought it," said the visitor.

"Fairy Ring Cottage was my father's, and now it's mine," said Charlie. "We live here. Our furniture was in the van."

"We like it," said Alice. "You needn't come inspecting us. We're happy here, after London."

"But surely you don't intend to stay? " said Mrs. Idris Evans. "They say such things about this place."

"Things have changed now," said Charlie. "We're here."

"And," said Alice, "we don't want to hear old tales to frighten the children just before bedtime."

"We do," said Tom, who did.

"He does," said Meg, who didn't as well as did.

Mrs. Idris Evans wrapped herself up again. "There will be problems when Fluellen comes back," she said. "It is still his house, and where will you be?"

"Fluellen was my great-great-uncle," said Charlie. "He won't be coming back. No problem. We're all happy."

"They say," said Mrs. Evans, "that all the stones in the circle outside were once people who meddled with the fairies."

"We don't believe in fairies," said Alice. "Do we?"

Only Meg couldn't say she was sure about that.

"It's not that pretty sort of fairies," said Mrs. Evans. "And all fairies are ethnically primitive, whatever."

"You bring one and we'll look at it," said Charlie. "Ha."

"Don't," said Hob. "Don't ask, Charlie."

Mrs. Evans put up the hood of her coat. "I'll be on my way," she said. "If you need anything my house is along the lane." She smiled sweetly at Meg and Tom, glared at Baby, and went to the door. She opened it and walked out.

Or did she open it? Hob was not sure. He heard her footsteps creaking across the snow, and then no more.

"If it is snowing like it is," he wondered, "why did she have only a few flakes on her coat? I'd like to know that."

"I felt funny when she looked at me," said Meg. "It wasn't like being looked at by a person."

"She is only a busybody," said Alice. "Inquisitive."

"Forget what she said," said Charlie. "I have."

Meg and Tom went to bed slowly. Last night had been fun. Tonight they thought of what they heard. Alice put a night-light on the landing. "It's only the wind in the snow," she said.

"I'm hearing it inside me," said Meg. "That's worse."

"Sleep well," said Alice.

Hob found footprints outside the porch. He followed them. Where the snow drifted right across the twisting path, where they should have been deeper, they vanished completely. But the snow had been brushed with something like a bundle of twigs. Twigs tied onto a shank are used for sweeping gardens, but have another use too. "She flew in, and she flew out," Hob said. "What does that make her?" He knew.

The children were saying, "Good night to Mom and Daddy, good night to Baby and Budgie. And good night as well."

"Who was that for?" said Alice.

"We don't know," said Tom. "We're not sure."

"They know Hob is here to keep them from harm," said Hob. "I must think what is good against witches, and do it."

He sat by the fire smoking his pipe. He found a blue dish full of pie, and ate it. It tasted of wood smoke.

"Like the old days," he thought. "If it wasn't for …"

He went round looking and listening. "I cannot prepare. Hob will fail. He cannot imagine how to stop goblins coming into the world. Hob does not know. Indeed I don't."

"They're welcome to the witch," he thought, taking up a piece of glowing charcoal and lighting his pipe.

In the morning there was a thick mist. It rolled along the kitchen floor stickily when the door was opened.

"It's coming up out of the well," said Charlie. "I never saw anything like this."

Hob listened down the well. He thought he heard voices.

The bucket came up with steam pouring off it. "It's warm," said Charlie. "It's hot. It can't be."

"This is not good," said Hob. "It is beginning."

Far off in the sky there was either a very large

black bird, or a witch upon a broomstick. He could
not tell.

SEVEN

hile Hob was sleep-
ing the next day there was a knock at the door. Alice
found two children outside, a girl and a boy.

"Have you come to play?" asked Alice. "I'll tell the
children. What are your names?"

The children smiled at her. They looked at one
another, and spoke quietly. The girl said, "What is a
name?"

Alice thought that was odd, but she was in an
unknown part of the country, and words might be different, that's all. "What do they call you?" she asked.
"But come in and I'll get Meg and Tom. Children," she
called. "Visitors."

The girl knew about her name then. "Rag," she
said, meaning it was her name. "Rag," she repeated.

The boy decided to tell his own name then. "Dew,"
he said.

"Those are our names," said the girl. "Rag, and Dew."

"These are Tom and Meg," said Alice. "Are you going to play indoors or outdoors?"

"We are going to make a snowman," said Tom. "You two make one each, and so shall we. The winner is the best one."

Hob woke a little. One of his senses told him the number of people had changed in a queer way. "Another Baby?" he wondered, and got up to look. There was the same amount of Baby, but four figures playing outside in the snow. "That's that," said Hob. "Or very nearly."

There were four snowmen by dinnertime. "You two had better run along home," Alice said to Rag and Dew. "I'm sure it is your dinnertime too." Rag and Dew did not want to leave. They did not want any dinner either, though they sat at the table. "Are you quite sure?" said Alice. "There's plenty."

They shook their heads and said nothing. They did not seem hungry. They did not look at the food on the table, as hungry people would. They sat solid and silent, smiling.

Tom's hands were very cold. He had to rub them together to make them work. He washed them in warm water.

"It's just as it came from the well," said Charlie. "I expect it's geology or geography, or something like that. Are there warm springs round here?" he asked Dew.

Dew said nothing, and only smiled more. When Alice suggested that their hands might be cold too,

Dew and Rag held their hands out. Alice looked at them, and felt them, and said nothing but, "They're clean."

She sat down and was very thoughtful. When the children had gone out to play again, she said to Charlie, "That was very strange. Those two children have hands like ours, but the fingers are joined together all the way, like the fins of a fish."

"I can't make out why they wouldn't eat," said Charlie. "Such a nice pie, too."

"It's a good little oven," said Alice. "But those are strange children. With those faces like little elves, but not so quaint. Thick, rather."

"Hob," called Budgie. "Hob. Come out."

"Bird's singing nicely," said Charlie. "Thinks it's home."

Hob heard Budgie. He got up, knowing the call was necessary from the voice Budgie used.

He came down quietly and asked what the matter was.

"Look out of the window," said Budgie. "What do you see?"

Hob looked. Tom and Meg had each built a snowman, tall and ordinary. But Rag and Dew had built snowthings, with thick arms and stout bodies, and skulls shaped like coal scuttles with ugly small countenances.

Hob was shocked at what he saw. He became visible, and Charlie and Alice saw him at the window looking out.

Meg and Tom had built things you could call men, like themselves. Rag and Dew had built something like themselves too. Dew and Rag were goblin children.

Alice was feeding Baby at the moment she saw Hob. Baby hung upside down for a moment, with a spoonful of apple climbing about his face. "What are you doing?" Alice asked him, wiping the face. "Charlie, did you see?"

"It was imaginary," said Charlie. "It can't have been there."

"Come on Baby, I didn't mean to feed you through your ear," said Alice. "I saw something horrid by the window."

Hob blushed with invisible shame. He wanted to go to his cutch, but he had to watch the goblin children.

"It's like the bus speedometer reflected in the windscreen," said Charlie. "And people walking through the fuel gauge."

"Open wide, there," said Alice to Baby. To Charlie she said, "What we saw was not in the windscreen of a bus. It was there between the table and the window. Wasn't it, Budgie?"

"Nup, nup, skwee," said Budgie. "Hob, up to his tricks."

"We're living in the country now," said Charlie. "We'll see all sorts of things we didn't know about."

"It'll frighten the children," said Alice. "Baby is howling."

"You are putting his dinner up his nose now," said Charlie.

"I wish Charlie and Alice would be quiet," thought Hob. "How can I think? And don't you start, Budgie," because Budgie had begun to hop about.

"I'm happy," said Budgie. "They've seen you like you really are, and they don't like it and you don't like it, and that suits me. I'm the family pet, not Hob."

"It's even upset the bird," said Charlie. "I'll put a cloth over it and quiet it."

That suited Hob very well. The bird stopped its noise at once. Hob sat on the cage under the cloth. He could peer out of the window and be visible, and still not be seen.

"They are spies," he told himself. "I could fight them. They have no swords. There is no danger of being cut in two."

He thought about goblin swords for a long time. Hob could allow most things to go right through him. He did not mind snow fluttering through. He did not mind rain wandering between his bones. Smoke came in and out as it wanted.

He would heal up as an ordinary sword went through. But goblin swords take centuries of work to come into existence, and more than one life goes into their making. In turn they take life, and a goblin sword could take the life of a Hob.

"A dwarf sword in my hand would be a match for a goblin," Hob thought. "But an ordinary sword, no. Goblin steel would tear through me, and I should die."

"Stop shuddering," said Budgie. "You're breaking the water in the pot and bending the cage. Baby will get in."

"I daren't think," Hob told Budgie. "And you can't. It's a pretty pickle we are in."

Budgie bit herself under the wing, and was very angry. But she dared not bring her head out.

"Even the bird is snoring," said Charlie. He and Alice were being quiet now, because they were almost quarreling.

"My wits are scattered," thought Hob. "Things are wrong. This is goblin work."

EIGHT

hings were wrong outside too. Meg and Tom had had enough of their visitors, but did not know it. They were looking at each other, thinking things like, "I hope he falls off the wall," or "She's no good at snow-down-her-neck, and I'll do it to her."

But really they were tired of the goblin children, and the goblin children were turning things that way. They never play.

"If you went in," said Tom, "then we three could play better."

"If you weren't here then we would enjoy ourselves," said Meg. "I don't know why I bothered to have a brother."

"I was there first," said Tom.

"I should have known from their names," said Hob. "Dew and Rag are not human names."

In the garden the words were coming more quickly,

and a true quarrel was beginning. The goblin children watched.

"I can't cure goblin quarrels," said Hob.

Dew was talking to Tom. Tom was looking wicked, and his eyes were creasing up small.

Rag was talking to Meg, and Meg's jaw was set very ugly.

"The touch of goblins is ruin," thought Hob.

Alice was looking through the window too. Hob might not know what to do, but Alice did. She rapped on the window, and four faces turned to look. Alice raised one hand and one finger on it, and they all stood still outside. Hob was sure that the snowmen and the snowthings had turned to watch too.

Alice went to the door. "Time to come in," she said. "Say good-bye to your friends, and perhaps they'll come another day." She said to Charlie, "Let's hope there are some nicer children soon. Including ours," she added.

Tom and Meg came in slowly, ashamed of being quarrelsome. "It is not their fault," said Hob. "But part of human nature is goblinish, so it will happen."

"You can help your Dad," said Alice. "It's much too cold out there." She did not tell them they were quarreling, or they would never have stopped.

"Great," said Tom; and Meg said, "Do we have to wash?"

"No," said Alice, and went on making a pie.

"I'll go to bed," said Hob. "It's high time. But I'll topple the snowgoblins first."

He went out again and set about the work. The afternoon light was blue, and so was the snow. Far away there were dark hills with snow on them. Black birds flew overhead, looking, calling, carrying messages. One of them, Hob knew, was not a bird, but a witch.

"Hob is not frightened of being hurt," he said. "He does not want to fail, that is all. I wish I knew what I could do. There is no one to ask. I am alone."

The goblin shapes had become statues of ice. Hob pushed and pulled until they rocked.

"I am too small," he thought. "I cannot grow until there is a desperate occasion, and this is just routine work for a Hob. I wish I did not feel so much dread when I am doing it."

While twilight crept up, one of the things creaked over in the snow. Hob waited for it to fall and break, but it leaned against the other one, and they stood together.

Hob went on working. At the moment of the sunset, something happened. The heavy snow changed under his hands. It began to feel like fur, like strong and eerie electricity. Hob's own hair rose on his head and his back.

"I did not know I had a back," he said. "I have not seen it."

The two snowthings softened to flakes and swirled round his head like something living. A puff of bitter wind blew across the garden, went through Hob like a goblin sword, and took the cloud into the air.

Hob looked, saw the shape the cloud made, and closed his eyes, terrified by what he saw. He knew this shape but dare not say the name. The cloud dispersed, and night came black over the garden.

"Day is over," Hob said. "Hob will sleep until midnight." He went to his cutch, fearing his dreams, terrified by reality.

"Pull the loose paper off the staircase wall," Charlie was saying. "Brush the wall, and I'll come to it very soon."

Hob tiptoed past, not understanding humans either. "Sometimes they are so tidy you daren't yawn; other times they do messy things like shaking rugs. I don't know what this is."

He went to bed and to sleep.

Tom pulled, and Meg pulled, and took off big strips of paper.

"I like this," said Meg, busier and busier.

"There's a little door in the wall," said Tom, in the corner of the kitchen.

"A cold draft is coming from it," said Alice. "I can feel it."

"No wonder they papered over it," said Charlie. "We'll have to do the same."

Tom and Meg put their fingers in the big crack and pulled. The door opened. Its hinges squealed.

Hob woke at the new noise. He was just overhead. "Are they here?" he said. "Have they found a way in? Is it too late?" He came down again to see what was happening.

Tom and Meg were looking into a black place alive with darkness. Tom put his hand in. Hob looked with him.

"Don't go in," said Hob. No one heard him.

"It's cold," said Tom.

"It smells," said Meg.

"Of goblins," said Hob. "Hob says paper it up."

Tom could feel steps going downward and wanted to follow them. "I'll take a candle," he said. "It must be a cellar."

"I didn't know there was one," said Charlie. "But it's the sort of thing Fluellen would have had."

Alice was rolling pastry. "Block it up," she said. "Cold is pouring from it and making Baby shiver and the fire smoke."

"We'll look first," said Tom. "And find the bones of Fluellen."

"You go," said Meg. "I don't want to find bones. Just bring back the crock of gold."

Charlie lit a candle, put it in a candlestick, and handed it to Tom. "Be careful," he said.

"Though I hate the smell of goblins," said Hob, "I'll go down with Tom."

"I feel safe," said Tom, feeling for the steps. "It's quite solid." He bumped up and down on the top step and the next one, and nothing gave way.

Tom was feeling for the third step down. "Give me the candle," he said. He drew it into the darkness with him. Its flame gave a gray light. Hob climbed in after him, clenching his teeth together so that they did not rattle. In the gray candlelight he dared to become visible.

He followed Tom, toward the noise.

"It's a cellar with music," said Tom, standing on the floor at the bottom of the stairs. "The music is very slow."

Hob had heard it ever since he arrived at Fairy Ring Cottage. It had been so slow and quiet he did not know it was a tune, played deep and low, on an instrument big as a county.

"Hob does not know music," said Hob. "I cannot tell tunes, and I cannot dance. What else is down here?"

Tom was disappointed. The music was dull and meant nothing. The cellar, in the shriveled glow of the candle, was small and square and empty, with stone floor and stone walls.

One wall was made of one stone. Hob knew it was the foot of the stone so like a door that Charlie had looked for the keyhole in it. "It is the door Fluellen opened to get into the goblin country," said Hob to himself.

"The music's out there," said Tom. "I don't know what it is."

Hob knew it was Fluellen's fiddle, playing for the goblin rout, keeping them busy until he walked through the door. He had been playing it beyond the door for a hundred years.

"Dad, I'm coming up," said Tom. "I don't like it here." He walked through Hob, and climbed the stairs.

"You were a long time," said Charlie. "You're just back in time for tea. What did you see in all that time?"

"I saw a little cellar, and came straight back," said Tom.

"It took you an hour," said Charlie. "But we could hear you down there, so we knew you were all right."

"Paper it over," said Tom. "It was creepy. There was someone the other side, coming through the wall, slowly. I'm frozen, and I was only down there a minute."

"Fluellen has been down a hundred years," said Charlie.

"Don't frighten the children with your nonsense," said Alice.

"We'd do best to return to London at once," said Hob.

"We're here," said Alice, as if she heard him. "Here we stay."

NINE

here was dinner ready for the table. Alice wanted to dish up.

"I don't feel hungry," said Tom. "I'll sit by the fire."

"You're chilled through," said Alice. She looked across at the little door in the wall. "It's a terrible draft coming in, Charlie, so please block it up."

Charlie only managed to put a chair in front of the little door, because at that moment there was a knock on the door.

Mrs. Idris Evans was there. "A nice fire is cheerful," she said. "What are you brewing up, Mrs. Grimes?"

"Our dinner," said Alice. She was uneasy at the way Mrs. Idris Evans arrived, first a thumping on the door, then the voice coming in, and Mrs. Evans being in the room without having to open the door much. Or perhaps at all.

"She's getting bold," said Hob to the pan of potatoes, which was what Alice was brewing. "She hasn't bothered to walk across the garden, or pretend to be anything but a witch."

In the old days people had a moat round the house. Nowadays people hung amulets over doors and windows. But either has to be done before the witch arrives. Once she is in you can only be careful.

"Alice does not know this is a witch, hoping for Fluellen," said Hob. He hunkered down behind the coal shovel.

"We were just about to sit down," said Alice, wanting rid of the visitor, thinking only about dinner.

Mrs. Idris Evans took a good look round. "Is the baby all right, in this damp old house, at a cold time of year?"

"He's very well," said Alice.

"Thriving," said Charlie, sitting firmly on the chair in front of the little door. "Country life suits him."

"I see you are decorating," said Mrs. Idris Evans. "You will uncover secrets under the old wallpaper, or under the floors."

"Yes," said Tom. He was about to say that if Charlie got up and moved the chair he sat on, then Mrs. Evans would see a secret of that kind. Hob did not want the witch to know about it. He had to stop Tom speaking without being seen himself.

"Are you there, Sootkin?" he called up the chimney.

"Yes," said Sootkin. "Fine smoke has returned."

"Speak up," said Hob. "Why are you whispering?"

"I'm not," said Sootkin, a little louder.

"What?" said Hob. "Are you there?"

"It's nice to talk with people," said Sootkin. "I'll shout."

"Gone out?" said Hob. "I can't talk if you go out. Come closer, will you?" Hob knew what he was doing.

Sootkin spoke louder. Alice thought it was a touch of sore chimney, but Hob's conversation was happening between Tom's word "Yes," and what he was beginning to tell the witch.

"I'm getting closer," said Sootkin.

"We found," said Tom …

"Closer," said Hob. "I can't come to you because of the fire."

"A little," said Tom …

Sootkin came to the foot of the chimney and looked out. "Where are you?" he asked.

"Just in time," said Hob. "Shake hands, please."

Sootkin put out a sooty hand. Hob held, and pulled hard.

Sootkin tumbled out of the chimney over the fire and the pan of potatoes. All the flue length of him came in a black slither, whooshing his long tail out across the hearth and into the room, where it fell like tar across the rug.

"Quick," said Alice, "Baby. Get him out of here."

"You were just telling me," said the witch to Tom.

Tom forgot what he had to say. He had a mouthful of Sootkin, and Sootkin down his neck.

Hob grabbed Sootkin's tail and threw it across the room toward the witch. She was so startled that she forgot to fill the clothes that pretended she was inside. Hob understood this very well. Sootkin's tail landed on her face, which wasn't there either, though it could be seen. Witches are meant to deceive, but sometimes they can be startled into forgetting it for a second or two. This was one of those times.

The tail fell through, and then down toward the ground. It dropped into the witch's boots, and began to fill her entirely. The rest of Sootkin followed.

Mrs. Idris Evans turned black as she stood there. She was angry, because she knew she had been out-witted. She tried to go through the door again, but now she was made of solid material she could not manage it. She had to open it for herself and walk out on her own, choked, black, and defeated.

For the Grimes family, there was only one small puff of sooty smoke, leaving a mark everywhere, but doing no harm.

"It's the wind," said Alice. "It puffed down the chimney."

"That's all," said Meg. "I'll help clear it up. Listen to the wind howling in the chimney."

"That's not the wind," said Hob. "It's baby Sootkins wanting their mother, but they're old enough to grow up without her."

Hob put his mark on the newly painted wall, with two sooty hands, little prints side by side. "Hob, his mark," he said. "The only word I write. Now I have been up long enough."

He went to his cutch and fell asleep. He woke

when the night was quiet, except for distant threads of sound from far below, something like singing in the ears. A little clearer, a little quicker, and it might have been music.

He got up and sat by the fire again for a while, sleepy with being awake in the day.

Something scratched and tickled up the cellar stairs and out into the room. It was a sharp creature, something between a ferret and hedgehog. Hob sucked his thumb where a tooth or a spike had made a hole. He opened the door and it went out into the night.

The witch's tracks were black across the snow. Candles burned at her house. She was scraping soot off, being cautious about water. Her cat Grim licked himself clean, blacker and blacker.

Fairy Ring Cottage huddled in the white landscape under the moonlight, and the great stones of the ring were black tusks encircling and eating the cottage.

"What can I do?" Hob wondered. "I wish it was not his job. I think I shall be hurt. But Hob will do it."

Small creeping things coming away from the house caused him to worry. They left strange tracks over the snow.

A band of elves peered out from the foot of a stone. They emerged shyly, and those behind handed up their belongings. The little things stamped their feet and blew on their hands.

Hob was sorry for them. What was to come had driven them into a cold world that no longer knew how to treat them.

An elf child spoke and the others hushed it. They picked up their bundles and walked on through the snow, over the ruts left by Meg's and Tom's shoes, house-hunting in the frost.

"We should go too," said Hob.

During his day's sleep he was woken by noise. Some was from Meg and Tom, and some from goblin children.

He saw Mrs. Evans approaching again. There was nothing he could do but watch. She watched back.

Tom and Meg saw her coming across the fields, riding her stick very low, so that she looked as if she was walking. She left the stick at the gate and came in on foot. Meg and Tom ran indoors, to tell Alice the visitor had come again.

They did not see the goblin children. One bowed to the witch, and the other curtsied. The witch was examining elf tracks in the snow. She turned and rode away.

"She's unreal," said Alice. "I hope she always turns back."

The goblin children went away quietly.

In the evening Hob sat by Baby. Baby was pleased. He could see Hob. He put out a hand to touch, and Hob held it.

"Uh guh," said Baby.

"That's right," said Hob. "Good Hob."

"Rubbish," shouted Budgie, scattering seed.

"It's a messy bird," said Charlie. "Christmas is coming," he warned her. "There's big turkey and there's little turkey."

"It's Hob," she shouted. But it was all in her mind, and the sounds were the usual nup, nup, skwee.

Hob played with Baby. Baby laughed. Budgie sulked.

"Such a nice house," said Alice. "Baby is so happy."

"But we don't like those children," said Meg. "Do we, Tom?"

"Not much," said Tom. "You can't get to know them. They kept changing the game they were playing."

Alice, busy feeding Baby, put a spoonful of spinach purée into Hob's mouth, and he choked invisibly but loudly. "I know you aren't there," she said, and patted his back.

TEN

ob climbed out of the cradle, Alice smiled, and Meg came running to see what was happening.

"Nothing," said Alice. "Moms can see things that no one else can. They can also pat them on the back if they choke."

"Shall I get him a tissue?" asked Meg.

"I'm off," said Hob. "To my cutch to recover. Tissue sounds like a sneeze, but it might be clothes too. If they give me clothes I'll have to go." For a moment more he stayed by the firelight, listening, being invisible as hard as he could.

Meg and Alice talked about Baby. They both knew that Hob was there, and were glad he was in the house.

"They are thinking of me," said Hob. "Hob is in their thoughts, and they know I am on their side. Hob must be careful not to think how frightened he is."

Baby was full of spinach. There was one spoonful left. Meg took it from Alice and held it out to Hob.

"I'll do it," said Hob. He reached out, took the spoon from Meg's hand, put it in his mouth, sucked the spinach from it, and gave the spoon back.

"Good for me," he said, "unless it gets up Hob's nose. But that's the same for most things he puts his nose into."

Hob went to his cutch for a little thinking and for what usually came next, a little nap. He thought serious thoughts. He almost thought the most serious thing of all, of what would follow the goblins who would follow Fluellen. He could feel it refusing to be thought of.

"Swords," he thought. "I know about swords. The dwarfs make swords, but there are no dwarfs here. They have been gone from the hills a long time now. The goblins drove them out. Swords are iron, and there is iron here. Tom and Charlie must make them, because I am unable to."

He was woken from his nap by footsteps above his head. The family was going to bed. It was time for Hob to be awake. He got himself up, and came back to the fire.

"Fire is in swords," he told Budgie. Budgie shrugged her shoulders at him. She did not bring her head out from under her wing.

"Swords are in fire," said Hob. "I have seen the work being done by dwarfs. There was much hammering and beating of metal. Hob knows about

HeadAche, but not about swords."

"I know about HeadAche, too," muttered Budgie, from her wingpit. There was no one in wingpit to hear.

"Hob is not meant to Think," said Hob. "I See and then I Do. I do not put things together to make sense. That is for humans. I have thought Swords; and that must be right."

Budgie sighed with impatience. She pulled her head out and looked round. She held her perch extra strongly. She opened her beak and squawked. She began to shake, and her cage round her.

And Hob wondered what was happening to him. Under his feet the earth ruffled its feathers, or something caught the spinning globe and made it tremble.

"Stop it," he said to Budgie, because she seemed to have begun it all. Then it was over. The shaking stopped, and the thing that had almost become a sound could no longer be heard. High on the roof a slab of snow shifted, creaked, slid and roared, and poured liquid into the garden.

Charlie sat up in bed. Baby sucked his thumb very loud. Meg and Tom turned over and went farther into sleep.

"Mmn?" said Alice. "Ibba bobba?"

"No," said Charlie. "Snow on the roof."

Alice put her head on the pillow and went back to a fluffy dream about new slippers for this cold house.

Hob looked at the fire. He was running through all the sounds he had ever heard to find what had caused the shake.

"It's It," he said at last. "That's what it was."

"Oh my goodness," said Budgie. "Just tell us what It is."

"It's walking," said Hob. "That's what It is doing. But what It is I don't know yet. It must be very bad indeed, or I would be able to remember what to expect."

"You just don't know," said Budgie. "Will you be quiet? Respectable people like to sleep at this time of day."

"It is putting Its foot down," said Hob. "It is walking. It is coming nearer."

"Don't wake me when it does," said Budgie. "Good day."

"Terrible day," said Hob. Whatever followed the goblins was within range. The next footfall would be nearer, and the next nearer still. One day it would be in the cellar, escaped from its proper world into this one.

"Hob has to stop it," said Hob.

Baby Sootkins were quiet. They thought a great wind had stirred the chimney. On the stairs Tread-Worm counted his segments, because dust had got in his eyes.

Hob said, "When the time comes I shall know what to do."

The moon looked through the window. Hob looked back. "When the next one comes," he said, "it will be Christmas. Perhaps Fairy Ring Cottage will not be here then. The family will be gone, and Hob will have come to an end."

Budgie shuddered, and Hob blinked, because across the moon some black thing flew, and called a mournful screeching call down to the ground below, full of longing.

"Vultures," said Budgie.

"Witches," said Hob, then changed his mind. "No," he said.

Something rustled up the cellar stairs and rattled against the little door. It pulled it open with a pluck and a scratch, and tumbled onto the kitchen floor, a tattered black bundle of shreds with no shape. A red eye looked round the room.

"Let me out," said its voice, weary and fearful.

"What are you?" asked Hob.

"We have been woken up and we are dancing," said the bundle. "The goblins are on their way."

"But you," said Hob. "What are you?"

"I am the first of the feathered things," said the bundle. "I have been asleep in the rocks, but the music has woken me."

"Yes," said Hob. "It has woken many things."

"It has woken worse than me," said the bundle. "Is this the world now? It is not large. Where is my other one?"

"It is flying," said Hob. "The world is outside."

Budgie stamped her feet. "Get it out of here," she said.

Hob opened the door. Hob saw something with a head like a newt, a body like a rat, and wings like a partridge. It stood on its own shadow in the doorway, covered with moonlight, woken from the rock once more.

"The big one is moving," it said. "We shall be extinct again."

It shuffled over the threshold, ran toward the moonlight, unfolded its wings, and lifted into the air. Its mate came swooping down from the moon, and they flew off together.

Under the house, far below, Something took another pace and set the cottage quivering once more. The forks sang in the drawer. Water in a bucket wrinkled and splashed. The fire had its ash shaken out, and glowed red again. A little Sootkin fell from its nest and slept on a hot ember.

"I cannot sleep for it," said Budgie. A moment later she was snoring.

Hob went to his cutch as if nothing was coming, nothing was threatening, nothing was trying to be thought of. He fell asleep with his mind wandering from ghost to dragon, from giant to thunder.

Sometime about the middle of the day he woke up and saw NightMare. He was perfectly awake and perfectly dreaming at the same time. He saw the thing he feared most, and knew what it was.

He had no idea how to deal with it. He had not met it before. "Of course not," he told himself. "I could not be here if I had. I would be over and done with, finished. There would be no Hob. I do not remember things I have not met. But this, this is a thing I know. What shall I do?"

He could not lie in his cutch and do nothing. He knew he must go down, become visible. and tell what he knew.

"But I cannot frighten them so much," he said. "Hob does not know what to do. If he does not tell, then no one will be ready. If he does tell, they will go away. But we all have to work together to beat this thing."

He came downstairs. Baby was having dinnertime down there. The others were eating sausages cooked in batter. Hob listened to what they were saying.

"No one will eat toads," he said to himself. "Hob knows that. How strange."

"There it is again," said Alice, because the house shook. In daylight the shaking was only like sunlight getting heavy and pushing. But at night, far down and deep, it weighed like a shadow.

Hob knew what it was now. He knew what was walking.

"I shall tell the children," he said. "They will tell Charlie and Alice, who will not believe me. They do not think I can talk. They think I should be swept from the house."

Hob went outside. The witch was not flying; Mrs. Idris Evans was not in sight. But two goblin children were tormenting a party of elves, heaping snow in front of them, putting footprints in the way so they had to go round because of the taint of goblin feet.

"None of that," said Hob. He put himself behind

one of the stones of the circle and made snowballs.
He began to throw them at the goblin children.

The goblin children stopped their unkind tricks and
looked round. One of them whistled.

"I know there are more," said Hob. "I know what is
following them. When dinner is over I shall speak to
Tom and Meg and tell them about the ..."

But at that moment a shadow fell on him, and on
either side of him there were teeth. The teeth were in
a huge mouth, and the mouth belonged to a goblin
dog that had seized him. It picked him up, shook
him, got its teeth firmly round him and carried him
away. It had him round the waist, with his arms fixed
so that he could not move.

He could only breathe slowly. He was unable to
speak. He was shaken again, headfirst into the goblin
dog's throat, ready to be swallowed. The dog began
to dribble on him, hungrily.

ELEVEN

The goblin children ran toward the dog, to join the hunt.

The goblin dog growled round Hob. It took tighter hold, and ran. Growling and gripping were painful.

Hob thought, "I don't feel pain unless I am meant not to. It tells me to stop feeling it. How? The dog is doing everything."

While the dog was running it stopped barking. But it went on breathing round Hob. The goblin children ran like puppets.

Inside the house Meg and Tom were finishing their dinners.

"Big dog out there," said Charlie. "What's running after it?"

"Snow lifting from the fields," said Alice. "No one is there."

"It's Rag and Dew," said Tom. "What are they doing?"

"Chasing the dog," said Meg. "It's got their toy."

Hob thought of everything but how to escape. The dog was not impressed by his skill. Its dribble and tongueyness and hot breathing were soaking him. His HobSuit was torn, and HobSkin as well.

Hob began to make himself smell disgusting.

Hob does not know everything. What is disgusting to him might be perfect for a goblin dog. It put Hob down on his back, sniffed at him delightedly, wiped its feet on him, and sat down puzzled, waiting for more orders from its eyes.

Hob was invisible in daylight. The dog waited to see what it had caught. In the dark it would have swallowed him. The stomach is quite content with invisible food.

Hob walked off like a crab. But he ran against the legs of the goblin children. They too were unable to see him, but they put their hands down and began to prod, to find the shape.

"They've caught something," said Tom. "What can it be?"

"I think they ought to stop it," said Alice, checking that Baby was still in the right place – the children outside were feeling for something that size.

"I don't know why they are playing in our garden as if they owned it," said Charlie. That was exactly what the goblin children thought about Tom and Meg.

The dog worked out that it was a waste of time to go on looking for something it only imagined. Just eat it now, it decided. Dogs are better at that than humans.

By the time Tom and Meg were outside, the dog was licking Hob the right way round for swallowing, and growling strongly at the goblin children.

It was a particularly ugly dog, with great jaws and a hard skull, more like a coal scuttle than a real dog. Its feet had an extra row of claws, and its tail ended in an arrow point.

Hob was desperate now. He had not got away when he was free of the jaws. It was time for any action that would help, no matter what happened later.

"Hob has one way to help himself," he said. "To be seen by daylight is better than to stop existing at all."

He closed his eyes, and made himself visible. The dog did not care. His mouth and licking tongue only felt things. The goblin children saw Hob and began to come after him themselves. He was a creature they could hunt down on sight.

Meg knew what Hob was. Tom knew. They had both seen him in the house.

The dog put Hob down, set a huge paw on him and turned toward Tom.

Tom was armed with snowballs. Meg carried a long stick like a spear. Hob lay face down, eyes shut, covered in dog dribbles. The dog licked the back of Hob's head, to make clear who was dinner and who was dog. Hob hoped it would be a quick meal, with no being eaten cold the next day and minced on the third.

Meg prodded the dog. It bit the end of the stick

off, chewed it, and spat it out as shavings. Tom threw a snowball, and the dog took no notice at all.

Then Charlie came out with an ax. He was intending to chop wood for the fire and did not even see the dog. The dog saw him, remembered about axes, and decided to leave without its meal.

It walked away, still proud, not beaten. It had only lost a meal of doubtful quality.

Charlie began to chop his wood. Meg knelt down in the snow and picked Hob up.

"Don't hang about," said Hob, with his eyes still shut. "Just a quick bite and a swallow. I'm not resisting. But it's not convenient, really. I have work to do, you know."

"It's talking," she said. "I heard words."

"Talking?" thought Hob. "This is the worst kind of dog."

"It's a sort of garden gnome," said Tom.

"It's real," said Meg. "I mean, alive."

Hob opened his eyes and looked. He found Meg holding him and Tom looking on. The goblin dog was away down the road, and the goblin children had left. "I'll take you in," said Meg. "I've seen you before."

"I'm sorry," said Hob. "I ought not to be seen. It would be better for me to walk and become invisible again. Then I shall tell you what has happened, and what will happen."

"Fortune-telling!" said Meg. "Perfect. I always want to know all about the future."

"Not this future," said Hob. "Especially." And with

that he vanished from sight, his way of becoming pale.

"It's gone," said Tom. "Did we imagine it?"

"I'm still here," said Hob. "Go back into the house. I must get dry of dog lick, and we could all do with a cup of tea."

Alice was still sewing. "Have your friends gone?" she asked.

"Yes," said Hob.

"Are you getting a sore throat, Tom?" asked Alice. "Go and wash your hands after playing with that dog."

In a little while Hob was saying, "I'd like to be invisible when I'm washing, please."

"We'll turn our backs," said Meg.

"You're both being silly," said Alice. "Aren't you?"

"I'll get dry by the fire," said Hob. "I have to tell you about the future. You will want to leave, I know."

"I think you are wounded," said Meg. "I'm the nurse and Tom is the doctor."

Hob thought, "Oh dear, she is beginning to play dolls with me. That will never do. Hob is not a play-thing or a toy human. I shall have to be firm from the beginning."

The ground shook under their feet; the cups hanging on the dresser sang like bells and touched one another; Baby woke and wanted to know things.

"What was that?" asked Meg. "Who did it?"

"That is what I have to talk about," said Hob. "It is real."

"It's like a big truck going past," said Tom. "In a tunnel underneath the house. But there isn't one."

"There is," said Hob. "Fluellen found it."

Hob went to sit against the fire to dry out his HobSuit. He lit his pipe for comfort. Charlie, who could smell a smoker on a bus, and extinguish him, wondered what wood was burning.

Alice put a cup of tea with a piece of cake beside it in the saucer, down in the hearth. Charlie supposed it was for Baby, but could not remember Baby drinking tea at that age, even when he was Tom or Meg.

He thought he was mistaken when cup and saucer were picked up empty and refilled before Baby was attended to.

Meg looked at her mother, and at the saucer. "It came with us," said Alice. "Don't alarm your brother or your father; men are frightened by such things."

Meg nodded her head. "True," she said.

It was bedtime before Hob could speak. He sat at the top of the stairs, on the family side, not underneath in his cutch. Meg and Tom sat up in their beds.

"It must be Fluellen," said Tom. "Dad's great-uncle. That's why we've got this house."

"It is our problem," said Hob. "Hob cannot do it alone. I do not know whether we can do it together. If we don't try, the world will be filled with true goblins. Those strange children are of the goblin kind. If you think about it you will know."

"Yes," said Meg. "They are different."

"They can be dealt with," said Hob. "Fluellen is

coming back. I have to deal with him. Hob is here, that is all. He is where he is. When Fluellen returns, the goblins will come after him, because he has taken the crock of gold. We shall have to fight them, not just a battle, but a war." He shook his head. "Hob believes he cannot manage that."

TWELVE

"If there's fighting," said Tom, "won't there be fighting back?"

"Yes," said Hob. "It won't be easy. Hob cannot think ahead. He does not know how. I do what I have to do, but only when the time comes. Hob was born before thinking began."

"You could try scratching your head like Daddy," said Meg.

Alice came up to say good night and blow out the candle. The thing under the ground moved another pace toward escape. Its foot hit the rock, and the shudder went through all the surrounding earth.

"There is no escape," thought Hob. Budgie was restless in her cage. Baby was wriggling in his cot. "They know something will happen," said Hob. "Hob will only remember what it is when it is too late." It filled him with gloom.

"It would be best to leave," he told himself. "Hob

can do no good. Alice and Charlie would think I was Indigestion, or Pain, and try to cure themselves of me."

He sat sadly by the fire. "I heard they had all gone," Hob told the poker. "But one is coming."

The poker fell off its little stand, rigid with fright.

Through the night the distant footfalls came at intervals. They went on through the next day, crunching through deep rock. "Geology," said Charlie.

Hob was asleep in his cutch by then. He did not see what happened during the day.

The family went shopping. Budgie stayed to keep the house in order. "There is a friendly spirit in the place," said Alice.

"Yes," said Meg. "We get on well."

"You can't like an old Hob," sang Budgie.

They shopped all the morning, and had their dinners in the town. Meg kept looking round and counting. "We're not all here," she said. "There should be another person."

"Granny can come for Christmas," said Alice. "And what about Mrs. Idris Evans? She needs company."

"It's not her that isn't here," said Meg. "Perhaps it's me."

Mrs. Idris Evans floated to Fairy Ring Cottage on her stick when the van had left, and skulked about, looking in the windows. Her cat Grim came across the scent of the goblin dog and went up to the roof.

"Seek and find, puss," said Mrs. Idris Evans. She saw the fire and heard Budgie practicing her low notes. She heard one of the footfalls, but took no notice of it. She knew only about Fluellen and the crock of gold.

"That Hob," she said. "I'll see him off before Fluellen comes back. That can't be long now, the witch-bone from my bat stew told me at Halloween."

The cat climbed to the ridge and stood there against the sky like a gargoyle. Goblin children saw it, and went back to their homes. The witch was not interested in them. She whipped them if they did not curtsey, to keep them in their place.

"It's all trouble, is a Hob," she said. "I smell the horrid thing. I'd like to drive it off. It ought to be exterminated."

Hob was fast asleep, dreaming of a witch coming close to the house, but not worrying. She would have to get much closer, he thought, before he had to do anything about it. His dream told him that. It also sealed the house against her.

She looked and she schemed. She tried the windows and tirled at the pin, she listened at chimneys and under the doors. She hunched herself under the eaves, seeking entry.

"Come back, Grim," she said at last. "We'll settle the pest."

She went home, and indoors, worked out what to do. Then she started to do it.

"Simples are always best," she said. "Plain old common sense, knowing the ways of the enemy. Not elaborate, but deadly, to get him out of the way for good. Or forever, because good doesn't come into it."

She sat between her fire and her window, contriving something while the day lasted. "A cruel trap," she said. "A sharp trap. To lay and to fell, to cast him off."

As she cut and put together, the Grimes family came back and took their shopping indoors. The biggest thing was a Christmas Tree.

"There will be no use for that," said the witch, at the last light in the window. "Now I have finished I'll wrap it up and take it across. One of those children shall do my work for me. Then we shall see how master Hob manages."

Hob slept until teatime. He got up, hoping he would get a cup of tea. But he also hoped he did not become too well known to Charlie and Alice. He ought to be a mystery to them.

"I don't want them to leave," he said. "I must put things right myself." It had come to him through all his dreams, a plan worked out and ready, but hidden from his mind, not ready to be thought. He heard the kettle boiling. He heard a knock at the front door.

"They can't come to play now," Alice called through to Meg, who was answering the door to a goblin child.

The goblin child's face was twisted with a smile. Goblins do not smile naturally. She said, "Ello Egg," because goblins are bad at words. "Iss iss or e ob."

Meg understood when the goblin child handed

over a packet with something soft in it. "I'll give it to him," she said.

"Esent," said the goblin girl, and curtsied to Meg as she would to a witch. She turned and went away. The witch was along the house wall. She held a pot of wasp honey for the goblin children to dip their fingers in, once each.

"Honey well spent," said the witch. "Come on, cat." She sped home through the twilight, Grim bounding across the snow below her.

"They'll have to learn when it's convenient," said Alice, coming through with bread and butter. "What is their mother about, letting them out at this hour of the night. Why, it's practically dark. They should be at home." She did not know what a goblin home was like; or that all the grown goblins had been dancing to Fluellen's music for nearly a hundred years.

The witch had put an unseeable Forgetfulness Stamp on the packet. It would stay out of Meg's mind until the right moment, and then the address would begin to work.

While Meg went to the door Hob talked to Baby, playing a game of catching Hob's finger. Hob made it visible, and then invisible, and Baby would grab for it. Then Hob did it with his nose, and then with an eye. Baby was as happy as possible.

Hob was not aware of anything beyond the cradle. He did not want to think about a resolve he had made, an action he had to take. He pictured the top cellar step, but quailed at the next one, though he knew he must soon tread it. He alone, he knew, must follow Fluellen. He alone must do something quite against his nature. Simply, Fluellen had not to return. Hob would have to see to it in the only sure way. No wonder he could not think it. That it would kill Hob too he had no doubt.

At bedtime Hob was sitting behind the fender, out of the way, and trying not to snore when he fell asleep, but not minding much because Budgie got the blame. "After all," he was thinking, "I am not doing anything bad to the dratted bird, nothing compared with what I shall do when I ..." His hard toes curled with a fearful desire to have the whole matter finished, himself too.

The address reminded Meg to fetch the packet and put it at its destination. She reached up under the stairs, to a little place she had not known about, and left the packet there.

Hob went to bed as the sun rose. "A little sleep," he said. "If I can manage it. Then I shall begin my plan."

He climbed to his cutch. There was something in the cutch already, a softish bundle, crackly with paper.

"A pillow," he said, feeling it. "Hob can manage a pillow."

He tried it as a pillow, but the knots in the string hurt his ears, and the paper crackled and woke him.

"It's a letter," he said. "Hob will open it. They are kind."

He opened the paper. He undid the string. Hob

likes a surprise present.

He folded the paper. He rolled up the string.

He spread out what was in the packet. "Clothes," he said. "Clothes! Hob will dress at once and be a fine figure in the world." He was delighted. He was proud.

He remembered nothing else; he forgot goblins and Fluellen. He forgot family and duty. Determinations and resolutions left him at once. What was beyond the cellar step no longer mattered to him. He ran his fingers along the pretty witching seams and tested the buttons, not knowing he was the buttonhole for their magical powers.

Now he had clothes he thought only of them. That's Hob.

THIRTEEN

"This is Hob's world,"
said Hob. "No wonder I could not sleep. This was
never a pillow. A weskit, a shirt, breeches, a cravat,
and a coat. White and silver and blue. And a hat!" He
jumped about in the cutch, and then under the stairs,
where there was more room. "Boots!"

"I must have forgotten to unpack," he said, when
he pulled a stocking on and admired his leg. "That is
not how Hob is meant to be. Hob should have
luggage."

He shook out the shirt. "Real buttons," he said,
doing them up with great joy. "I am on my way," he
sang. He did not care whether he woke everyone. He
had forgotten them all.

"Now the breeches," he said, pulling them up, and
putting the braces over his shoulders. "The right size
for Hob."

The house shook, and dust fell from the stairs.

"Help," said Budgie, trying to take her head from under the wrong wing.

"These clothes will get dirty and dusty," said Hob. "Why do I stay in such a place at all?"

He tied the cravat. He slipped the weskit on and fastened twelve buttons. "Luxury," he said. "Civilization. It's proper." He spoke to himself firmly. He did not want to remember that the shaking meant the approach of something deadly.

"Goblin Kings," he said. "Fairy tales." But his voice sounded strange, because until now he had not thought the words Goblin King even in his dreams. But he was bound to know that after the goblins came their king.

"Nonsense," he said. "The goblin king will not come out as large as a house and start destroying all he sees, eating men, women, children, cats, dogs, hobs." He shook his head. "What a deal of nonsense there is in my mind." He pulled the points of the weskit, and it sat snugly round him. "A lot to be said for a good tailor. Now for the coat."

He put an arm in, and then the other, and held the collar up and forward, and the coat was round him, warm and well-fitting, still stiff with newness.

"Fits like a ... glove," he decided, and felt in the pockets and finding a pair of them. "I'm ready," he told the cutch.

He thanked no one; he did not say good-bye. He slipped out of the front door and set out across the snow. He was gone.

"Who could want to be out in the middle of nowhere like this?" he said. "There can't be anything to do. Nothing of importance here." But his voice faltered a little, not quite sure of what it was saying.

"All nonsense," said Hob firmly to a signpost. "Which way to London?"

The signpost pointed all its ways at once, and gave no help. There was only writing on it, and Hob has always thought that reading would lead to problems.

Fairy Ring Cottage lay under the cold moon, its windows dark. Round it the stones were stark in the snow, so much blacker than night that in any darkness they would still be visible.

With every mile Hob went he remembered less of the cottage, and the people in it melted from his mind.

He came out of the snow and went down a valley. "When I get among better company I shall forget them entirely," he said. "I must have eaten human food that did not agree."

And in a mile or so more, "What can a Hob do for humans? They are a different race. We can't be useful to each other. I'll live in town and be my own master. I've the clothes, the time, and the nature to do it well; handsome, well-dressed, of a very good family, I should do well. I don't wish to be among country bumpkins. Good-bye to all that, and good-bye again."

Mrs. Idris Evans sent her cat to sniff for Hob. The cat followed Hob's tracks, knowing the pattern in the boot heels.

"Well done, Grim," said the witch. "We'll go across and see what they know; and what they don't know, too. Then it will be time. I have tamed the goblin children already, and soon I shall tame the grown ones. They will all do as I want. I have waited many years for the moments that are coming."

The cat went to sleep. He did not see that his life would change. He did not want to be a human. He thought humans had some unhygienic disease, and had lost their fur. But it seemed to be the fashion for cats to have them around. Mrs. Idris Evans sat at her window and waited. Something would show the moment was right for the goblins to be taken over. She thought of millions of them curtseying to her.

In Fairy Ring Cottage Meg looked around for Hob. There was nobody behind the fender, or under the table. Baby looked for his friend who sometimes had an eye, sometimes a finger, or a nose; or, as a special treat, a smile only.

"He's gone to bed," said Meg.

"Stop talking nonsense," said Charlie.

"I can tell he is not here," said Tom. "The house is empty. He must be outside."

But outside was empty too; the garden was quite bare of any sense of Hob, like the kitchen, the back room, the stairs.

"Just not here," said Meg. "We were getting on so well, too. I wonder if it was that parcel. Has he seen it?"

She went to look, climbing up under the stairs and reaching into the cutch.

The packet was not there. There was well-slept-on mouse nest. There was brown paper lying folded neatly. There was string. The cutch was Hobless. It was a cutch no longer, only a hole under some floor-boards. Hob had gone.

"Why?" said Meg. "What did we do wrong?"

Charlie said, "Stop crying into your cornflakes, Meg. They'll go limp and soft and you won't be able to eat them."

"Hush, Charlie," said Alice. "It's just one of those days. It's the weather, I expect."

"It's one of those lives," said Meg.

Crunch, shudder, came a shaking, nearer and sooner, closer and louder.

"We seem to be approaching the road or the railway, Charlie," said Alice. "Or it's coming to us."

"Don't be silly," said Charlie. "You can all go home if you don't like it here. I shall stay, and that's that."

Meg sniffled into the cornflakes again, pushed the bowl away, and went to sit on her bed, busy looking after herself.

Several miles away, with the sun sending a long shadow in front of him, walked Hob. He did not know which road he had taken or what he should do. He knew only that he must not go back to Fairy Ring Cottage. To be fighting goblins was quite wrong for him. Thoughts of dealing with Fluellen were idle.

"Only as big as a smallish house, a goblin king," he told himself. "No worries about, no need to do anything about it."

He sat on a milestone, knowing other things about goblin kings. "They've got to eat," he said presently. "Naturally." He pretended he did not know perfectly well that any tender person was their chief delight, bones and all.

"Just natural," he said again. "The same as it's natural for me to be well dressed, on my way to London, without a care in the world. That's where I'm going." He whistled a jaunty tune, but it bent in the middle and drooped, flat as mud.

"I expect Hob is getting a blister," he said. "That's why I don't want to walk any farther."

He took off his new boots and looked at his feet. There were no blisters. "I knew," he said. "I shall walk on."

He walked through the night. It was weary traveling for him and for the road too. Going uphill put a great strain on it.

The road rested at the top for a short distance. Hob looked back. The rays of the rising sun picked out Fairy Ring Cottage like an unlucky jewel. Hob's heart turned in its socket.

"But I'm free, I'm enjoying myself," said Hob. "That's what I'm doing. Hob is happy." But he was not free because he had to wear clothes, not happy because everything was wrong.

"I'll go back," he said. "And fold the clothes up and put them back in the wrappings. That's what Hob will do."

He turned in his tracks, but before he had taken

ten HobStrides he found blackness settling in round him.

Hob gasped and struggled. He found air and daylight again. A huge agony came into his head, because he should have forgotten where he had been. He should not care. "Hob is made to forget," he said. "I am not in that world now."

He walked on, down the far side of the hill. The Grimes family and their house went out of sight.

"My nose runs," he said. "That never happens to Hob. Is it raining? Why are my cheeks wet?"

FOURTEEN

The road became old and rough. Time had gone back and Hob walked in an early wild place, beside a little river. He had a new feeling as well. When he lived in a house he hardly needed to eat. Food was an extra then. Now it was necessary.

"Just hungry. Particularly hungry. Why is Hob's mouth watering? Can he smell something? Yes, I can."

He could smell bacon, mushrooms, new bread, butter, pepper, salt, tea, milk, honey, marmalade. The smells grew stronger. Somewhere along the little river breakfast was making. A little breeze brought aromas along.

There was a painful cry from behind his weskit. "Yes, yes," said Hob, "we are going there, whatever it is." He followed his nose up the breeze.

An encampment of people his own size was finishing the breakfast, wiping plates clean with hunks of bread.

"I'm too shy to speak," said Hob to himself. But down behind his weskit they did not care. "Go on," they said. "Ask."

Hob thought, "Politely, remember," and stepped forward.

Bearded faces turned to look at him. The jaws under them were still eating. Hob had come upon a Company of dwarfs. The thought of breakfast absolutely cleared his mind of something that had been bothering him – some dream about a house with dark stones round it; nonsense about goblins.

"Vanish," he told it. "It is broad daylight, another place, another time, and Hob, why Hob is someone else now."

The dream vanished. Hob had forgotten Fairy Ring Cottage. It was the right moment for doing so. Dwarfs search your mind and find what you really intend. Hob only intended something to eat for now, and thought of nothing else.

The dwarfs searched his mind. In a matter-of-fact way they stacked their plates, drained their mugs, emptied the teapot of leaves, and buried the fire with turf.

They said nothing. There was no breakfast left, so no one could have it, and welcome. They wiped their beards, hitched their loads up on their backs, and walked on up the river.

Hob stopped. There was disappointment behind his weskit. The Company was going out of sight in a long line. One knapsack was left in the encampment. No dwarf had picked it up. The last dwarf looked at it and at Hob.

"They want me," Hob decided. "I am to carry that knapsack."

He went forward, picked up the knapsack, and began to hoist it on his back. It was very heavy. He was out of breath before he had walked an inch. The last dwarf waited for him, then led the way. Hob followed.

Before long his back and shoulders were making more fuss than his stomach had. His legs began to ache. A button popped off his coat and disappeared. His stockings fell asleep.

The Company came out of the woodlands and strode uphill to the moors. They crossed mile after mile of moorland, mire and grass, heather and gorse, until they came to the bare rock of the mountains. They stopped again, and dropped their loads. Hob knew they would have tea. But they did not. They grumbled for a time and set off again.

The stars came out. The sky went dark, and the sound changed about Hob's ears. They marched along a road now, smooth and clear, through darkness as dark as the complete darkness Hob had been in when he tried returning to ... well, he knew he knew where, but did not want to think it.

He thought he saw daylight ahead, but it was a small candle, smelling deliciously of roast lamb. Hob saw he was in a rocky tunnel. The dwarfs laid themselves down and went to sleep. Hob was about to do the same, but the dwarf with the longest beard wagged it and meant, "Keep watch. Wake me if."

Hob sat by the candle. He did not sleep, but long dreams came to him. The candle ate itself down to a puddle of tallow, then went out in its own gravy. There was wreath of smoke, and then darkness full of snoring. Hob could see now whatever he thought about: Baby; the bright house with stairs and the Gremlin that drove it away; Meg and Tom; goblin children; Alice handing down a cup and saucer and cake; his own cutch (he longed most for that); himself, parading smartly through the world, being served breakfast – though that was a big fancy that never happened.

He saw the goblin king clear on the darkness. He woke at once, just as the dwarfs began to stir from sleep.

Hob thinks he marched the next day asleep. He next knew that his neck hurt because he was snoring on a hard pillow. First he blamed his cutch, until he found he was not in it.

"Hob has fallen out," he said. He smelled breakfast again, and his stomach writhed. He blinked at a bright light, and found it was firelight. "Hob has fallen into the fender," he thought, and looked up to say something to Budgie.

He was in a cave, after all, among dwarfs. He was nudged into line and had a dish in his hands. He had breakfast put on it, and sat by the fire to eat it.

There was as much to eat as he liked. His weskit

grew tight round him, and he undid the buttons. Then the plates had been wiped clean, the fire put out, and hands were helping him put a knapsack on his back. The walking started again, in darkness.

After a time there was light ahead. The Company came into a factory cut from rock, full of fires, where dwarfs worked with hammers and hot metal.

Hob thought, "Swords. Swords are needed for the goblins and for the goblin king."

The dwarfs turned to look at him, to remind him that he should not think of a past he had left or a future he had lost.

He had to work. He was expected to understand when he was given a bag of charcoal to burn, a piece of iron to hit, or a basket of onions to peel. His turn to pump the bellows was the hardest work. When he felt most weary from that he had to watch while the Company slept.

For many nights he still saw goblin kings on the darkness, saw goblin children, ached to return to Fairy Ring Cottage. He tried not to think such things, but could not help it.

One day his coat was not on his back, because he had left it hanging beside the bellows. He did not find it. He was glad that it no longer held him in its arms.

The Company moved about the cave, with different things to do as they went. At first lumps of iron had been made white hot and beaten into a strip. Farther on the strips were baked in charcoal for many days, then taken white hot to an anvil.

Here they were hammered longer and longer, and folded on themselves. It was like Alice making puff-pastry, Hob thought. The strips were beaten and fold-ed again and again, then plunged into the stream that thundered through the cave.

After that there was a workshop where things were made of wood and leather, then another workshop with brass and silver, and one where gold was fashioned.

At the end the dwarfs had made swords. They rested on a rack in their leather scabbards, gleaming with gold.

"Why?" thought Hob. "Why indeed? All the dwarfs have swords already." He recalled that he needed a sword, and that he needed it soon. He wanted more than one, because ... his memories had begun to fade. He could hardly remember why he wanted three swords, or that he wanted them now.

"But he must indeed have them," he said, "and at once."

That night it was his turn to watch. When every dwarf was asleep he got up from his place and went to the rack of finished weapons.

He picked one up. It hung new in his hands, never used, not named, fresh and sharp. He took another, all the time wondering what he was doing, but know-ing that he had to. "The first for me," he thought. "The next for ..." But he could not find Tom's name. "And a third, for luck."

The swords jangled, and each one moved in its scabbard. Hob took off his shirt to wrap them.

He began to follow the only road he knew, the way he had come in with the Company. He went past workshops and furnaces, into the tunnel.

"Hob will become invisible," he said. But invisible in the dark does not work. People listen more intently.

Hob stumbled on the edge of the road and dropped his load.

Behind him there was a shout, and the raising of lights, and the noise of running feet.

FIFTEEN

t Fairy Ring Cottage Budgie sang out an insult. "Your mother was frogspawn," she trilled.

"I wish that bird didn't always say 'Nup, nup, skwee'," said Charlie. "I get bored with the same thing day after day."

Budgie had been missing Hob. She hoped he would answer an insult. But Charlie thought all her insults were the same.

"They're different," said Budgie. "What about the one that says he is related to a gumboot?"

"Let's have some variety," said Charlie. "Sparrow."

The house was shaking more and more often, swinging Budgie's cage, hardening sugar in its jar, raising dust.

"It's coal mining," said Charlie. "One of those things."

"There's no one to look after us," said Meg.

"One day he was here," said Tom. "Then he wasn't."

"We've given up imaginary friends," said Charlie firmly, and Alice sewed quietly, not looking beyond the tail of her thread.

Mrs. Idris Evans came one day. Two goblin children curtsied. Mrs. Evans knocked on the door.

"Any little problems?" she asked. "You will let me know, won't you? Nothing left by the last tenant?"

"All we have here we brought with us," said Charlie.

"No little people round the house?" asked Mrs. Evans.

"Nothing worse than ourselves," said Alice.

"It worked," said Mrs. Evans to Grim, on the way home. "The little busybody left." She saw a scrap of paper pinned on the gate. Meg had written, "Come back, Hob. We want you."

Mrs. Evans looked hard at the paper until it was a cinder.

Alice still put down cups of tea and pieces of cake. But she had to take them up afterward.

"You're attracting mice," said Charlie. "Or worse."

"That witch brought that present for him," said Meg, thinking of Hob. "Do you think he's gone to live with her? I don't think that would be fair."

And Baby cried because Hob was not there to play with.

*

Hob had been in underground places before. There had been red trains, but nowhere for a cutch, because the stairs had never stopped moving long enough to make a top step.

"Hob makes a plan," he said to himself, "but does not know what it is, or which way to go, and he can see nothing."

He heard the clatter of dwarf boots behind him, and saw the spark of metal on rock. Ahead there was darkness, but what pursued him might be worse.

Behind him the dwarfs were holding lanterns. The light they used to find him by helped him to get away.

"Am I better off, or worse?" thought Hob, because the faster he ran, the faster the dwarfs followed. At last he could run no farther, and stopped.

"Hob will fight," said Hob. "I have the weapons." He faced the dwarfs, and breathlessly pulled a sword out.

No dwarf came near him. They stopped as he drew his sword. They knew about the edges of their own blades.

"I shall walk after all," said Hob. "I shall walk out of this underground place."

He began to see something ahead that was not reflected lantern light. He saw steady points of light against darkness, and felt colder air coming on his back and chest.

He set his hat on straight, untwisted his braces, stamped his boots, straightened his stockings, and walked on.

He was walking on grass, through rough stems, and over snow. "Hob is outside," he said. "The light is from the stars. I have come out from the dwarf country."

He looked round. There was empty moorland ahead, and mountain behind. The cave mouth was a deep shadow. Hob climbed up and sat above it.

Very soon a Company of dwarfs came out, lanterns swaying, swords shining, boots thumping. They went straight on, over the moor, and out of sight.

Hob came down and set off in another direction. He understood stars, and Fairy Ring Cottage was over that way.

By moonrise he was at the edge of woodland. By daybreak he was beside the little river, and before longing for sleep he was at the little bridge.

"I'll cross now, and then perhaps rest," he thought. "I am clear of dwarfs."

He was on the bridge when he saw something else on it too, facing him. It was a dwarf. He fumbled for one of his three swords, but dropped them all. He bent to pick them up and a second dwarf fell over him from behind. A third came up over the parapet of the bridge and joined in. Dwarfs quarrel with anyone. They busily fought each other for a moment.

Hob got away with the swords, but lost the shirt they were wrapped in. A dwarf threw it into the water.

He hurried up the road to the top of the hill. In his haste a boot came off, worn through with hard work. It tumbled back down the hill.

At the top he sat down on a rock, worn out. A beam of sunshine came walking up from ahead of him and caught him in its warm lick.

Hob took off the other boot. He pulled off both stockings and put them in the boot. He hurled the boot toward the bridge. It walked down, tump, tump, tump.

"Happier with its mate," he said "I'll be happier at Fairy Ring Cottage. I can't get back with my clothes on. How do I lose hat and breeches? They still hold tight."

He went on cautiously, remembering how the world had turned black and strange last time he tried returning. He made sure of each footstep before his weight was on it.

A goat in a field saw a good edible hat wandering along the far side of the hedge. She put her head over, waited for it, and took it. Hob did not notice. The goat chewed steadily on.

Hob's way became clearer. He was only wearing breeches now, and he could go where he wanted, but was unable to do more than look after himself.

"I don't do much at the best of times," he said. "Hob is too small and insignificant. I might as well not be there."

He turned a last weary corner, and in front of him was a tall stone, black as starless night. Behind it stood more, and among them was Fairy Ring Cottage.

"Two more hedges and two more gates," said Hob, thinking only breeches were the problem. But the dwarfs were close behind him, in an ugly mood.

"Stop, thief," said one. And with his own dwarf sword he cut Hob's braces so that his breeches fell down round his ankles and tripped him up.

"Later," called Hob, and began to escape straight through the hedge, struggling and straining, pricked by spines, hooked by thorns, torn by HedgeTear with his brambling spikes.

He went through one hedge, and the next. He was in Fairy Ring Cottage's garden, and had got home. He hurried across the garden. But something felt odd. He looked down, and found that the hedge had torn his breeches from him, and he was in his own HobSuit now. He felt stronger and more real.

"I am Hob again," he said. "I hope I am not too late. The house is still standing."

He went to the door and tried the catch. He could not move it. He felt for a loose window. He climbed up on the roof and looked down a chimney. He could not enter.

"Locked out," he said. "What shall I do? This is my home."

"You will never get back inside," said the black cat Grim. "You have been sent away. You are not welcome anymore." He hurried to his mistress to tell her Hob was back. Wicked footprints dabbed unfriendly messages faintly on the snow.

Inside the cottage a family decision had been taken, one for and four against. The four against knew they would lose.

"That's settled," Charlie said. "Unless the Budgie wants to come outside and fight about it. We'll leave in the morning. We're too sensible to tough it out. We'll go."

SIXTEEN

ob went round
and knocked on the door, rapping firmly.

"Go away," called Charlie from inside. "It's that old
woman from up the road, or those children, always
hanging around."

"I won't go away," said Hob. "But I must be invited
in."

The ground shook.

"It is near," said Hob. He looked at his three
swords, and at himself, uselessly smaller than Tom or
Meg. "It is too late. The goblin king will get out. It is
the end of happiness."

The cottage door opened. Alice was saying, "Now,
you three stay out of the way. We're packing to leave,
and that's that. Don't go far, and wrap up well."

The pram came as far as the door and stayed there.
Meg went back for a hat, and Tom was hardly ready
at all. Baby was half in, half out of the doorway.

Hob climbed up and into the pram. Baby was glad to see him. "A piffle a glob," he said.

"I know," said Hob. "And the same to you." He put his thumb out and showed it to Baby. He showed an eye, and Baby laughed. Baby held a toe twinkled at him. Baby pulled. Hob pulled. But Baby pulled harder.

"Ith poff," said Baby, pulling the toe right up to his mouth and putting it in.

"Ow," said Hob. "Those are teeth, you know."

Then he realized what Baby had said. "Ith poff" meant "Come in," and it was as simple as that. Baby meant to pull Hob's foot from outside the house to inside the house, where the mouth was. Hob was inside.

"Thank you, Baby," said Hob. "Bite me if you want."

Baby laughed. He chewed Hob in a friendly way.

"I must bring my luggage in," said Hob. He went out and picked up the three swords. He took them to the little cellar door and put them inside. "They'll be ready there."

And the ground shook.

"Yes," said Hob, "you can do that as much you like, but we shall be ready for you."

Budgie swung upside down, twisted her neck, and looked at Hob. "Is it you?" she asked. "Hoped you had left home."

"This place is still like a henhouse at times," said Hob.

"Did you like the clothes she sent you?" asked Budgie. "You didn't show them to me."

"So that's what happened," said Hob.

He saw a dwarf's beard moving beyond the hedge.

Tom and Meg wheeled the pram away. "It's been a holiday," said Tom. "Don't be cross."

"I was just getting to like it," said Meg. "But I'm cold all the time. My nose is red." They closed the door after them.

The hedge was full of dwarfs, uneasy about humans.

Charlie came downstairs with a box. "That bird twittering on again," he said. "Why don't we leave it here when we go?"

"It sings pretty loud," said Alice. "But it's company."

The floor shook again.

"So's that," said Charlie. "That's staying, if nothing else."

Hob decided never to go out again. "If the goblins don't get me the dwarfs will," he said, deciding never to stay in either. "Or the goblin king. Even if he spits me out that's too late."

The cutch was full of empty wrapping paper. He saw from a bedroom window the hedge full of swords glittering in sunlight. He came down and sat in the fender. The floor shook, the fire irons sang, and Budgie made faces at her mirror.

Meg and Tom came back, and Baby with them. "Not comfy outside," said Meg.

"The hedge was staring," said Tom.

There was tea. Every five minutes now a long
trembling shake made the candle smoke.

A cup of tea came down, a chocolate biscuit in
the saucer.

"I wonder if we need leave," said Alice. She was
feeling more comfortable now, without knowing why.

"I'm not changing my mind every five minutes,"
said Charlie. "We're going. It won't do here."

Hob took the cup and saucer. "Why?" asked Alice.
"I've forgotten why." She felt safer now Hob
was back.

The floor shook.

"That's why," said Charlie. "The house will
be about our ears any moment. People get killed
that way."

"That's nice," thought Hob, sucking melted
chocolate from the edge of his biscuit. "The goblin
king is going to kill Hob, and when he has he'll come
to London and get you all. How is it that you don't
know about goblins and their kings?"

"I hear the kettle singing," said Charlie.

"It'll be mice in the ashes," said Alice. "They love
it here."

The floor shook again. Hob's cup had a waltz round
his saucer and decided to go home alone. Hob res-
cued it and sent it up for more, and another biscuit.

The distant singing sound had become quicker.
Hob could follow the tune, distinct and near.

"Fluellen playing the violin," he said. "That's what."

"Music," said Charlie. "Unnatural. The house is haunted."

"It's not haunted," said Meg. "Really it isn't. That's Hob. It is Hob, isn't it, Tom?"

"That isn't," said Tom. "That'll be Fluellen."

"Fluellen playing the violin down there to the fairies," said Meg. "Listen, ta de da-te diddle-um, teedle-eedle-impety."

"Well, what's that shaking that comes every few minutes?" asked Charlie. "Fluellen's heartbeat? He didn't have a heart. He was just a mean old miser."

"That runs in the family too," said Meg.

"I'll have to speak," thought Hob. "I will." So he said aloud, "It isn't Fluellen."

"That bird," said Charlie, jumping up in fury. "I can't bear it. I'll nup nup skweeze its neck and settle its nonsense."

"I never said a word," said Budgie.

"Shut up," said Charlie. "What were you saying, Tom?"

Hob said, "I'll become visible, or he won't believe me." He sat on the fender and tried to become visible. "It's not working," he said after a time. "I can't see me. Can anyone?"

"The coal is haunted," said Charlie.

"Oh Dad," said Meg. "Just listen. That's Hob."

"I think I'll go for a walk," said Charlie. "I'm going mad cooped up in here."

Hob was in the middle of the pain of becoming visible. "I expect I'm nervous, that's all." He tried again. "I manage it for Baby, so why can't I manage it for Charlie?"

He went to sit on the edge of the cradle. Baby knew he was there. Hob may be invisible, but he is heavy for his size. The cradle swung a little. Baby smiled. Hob showed him a thumb.

"What is that nasty floating thing?" asked Dad. "That's a bad habit in babies. Get a tissue and remove it, please."

Hob put a whole hand up, and then an arm, and gradually made the rest of himself visible.

"I keep seeing it," said Charlie. "I've gone mad. I must be mad. It's the only explanation."

"We've all seen him," said Alice. "He was playing in the snow with the children the other day."

"Fluellen is coming back to this world," said Hob. "He has not eaten a thing down there, so he has not had to stay. But goblins will follow him, because he has stolen their crock of gold. They're bad enough; but after them comes the goblin king, big as a house. He lives on human heads. We shall fight the goblins first, and then deal with the king."

There was silence. "He talks a lot for something that isn't there," said Charlie. "All the more reason to leave, I'd say."

"There are swords," said Hob. "But their owners are outside waiting to get them back. And don't forget the witch. We have big problems all round."

Down below there was a rumble like a falling wall.

"They're coming." said Hob. "We have to be ready."

Charlie looked round in amazement. "I believe it," he said. "I don't know why, but I do. I'm no good with a sword, but I have a lovely sledgehammer in the van. I'll get that."

"If you see anything," said Hob, "hit it. They're all on the other side now."

"What?" said Charlie. "I didn't hear."

"We didn't say," said Alice. "But we meant Be Careful."

SEVENTEEN

hey were always coming up," said Tom. The cellar floor had been crossed by tiny paws, and the stairs climbed by them.

"Mice, elves, and other things," said Meg. "Families."

Hob knew about families. This one was his own again. He stood and waited with them. His sword was his own length. Beside him Meg and Tom were large.

"You are magic," said Meg, hoping he was.

"No," said Hob. "I see other things, that is all. My life is a slightly different kind, but just as confused as yours."

Elsewhere other things happened. Charlie went to the van to get his sledgehammer. Before he laid his hand on it he felt something sharp at waist level. He saw three bearded dwarfs, scratched by thorns. Swords flashed in torchlight.

"What do you want?" said Charlie, in a squeaking voice.

Alice heard another rumble down below. It was too much. She picked Baby up, wrapped a tablecloth round him, flinging cups onto the floor, and went out into the night.

"Charlie," she called. "Where are you?"

Charlie said, "Gee-euk," in reply, because a sword cut a piece of his shirt out, by the tummy button. Gooseflesh ran down his spine and bristled the backs of his hands.

Alice saw Charlie's light by the van. In fields an unknown light, greenish and smooth, glowed on the snow, sliding behind hedges and gliding through gateways.

There was a third light as well, far down the valley. She thought it was a truck, grinding up the hills, lights wavering wildly but coming steadily on, vanishing as the road bent, and with a roar of engine and howl of gears appearing again.

There was candlelight coming from the house windows. There were figures moving in the garden.

"Come on, you two," said Alice. "Of course we can't stay. Come with me and get into the van. We'll have to go at once."

The two children followed her, saying nothing.

"No good sulking," said Alice. "You can't go back in the house for anything. Feel lucky to have got out at all." She hurried the children along with her.

Charlie flashed the light on them.

"Those aren't our kids," said Charlie.

"They're somebody's," said Alice. When she looked

she saw goblin children. She hastily uncovered Baby, and found that he, at least, was hers. The dwarfs surrounded all of them.

"Get in the van," said Charlie. "These monkeys don't know English. I don't think they're even human."

He saw the greenish light, not far off. He heard and saw the truck, or whatever it was, hastening along the narrow road.

"It might be a tank," said Alice. "Heavy rescue ..."

"It sounds like, ..." said Charlie. Then he turned on the dwarfs. "Give up tickling with that poker, shrimp, or I'll lay the jack handle on your ear."

A sword went into his hip, and grated on the bone. It hurt surprisingly. Blood oozed out.

"Now listen to me," said Alice, knowing how to speak to little people even if they had swords. "Behave. Pay attention."

At Fairy Ring Cottage the light began to come out of one of the walls in a dazzling strip. All round, standing stones were filling with the same light, like crystal lit from below.

In the cellar one candle on a shelf in the wall gave a roomful of light and a roomful of shadow.

Beyond the walls there was the continual tread of huge feet, distant but approaching. "My heart beats that fast," said Tom.

The shadows began to shift. The wall that was a single stone let daylight through, but not the day of the known world.

"Do some magic," said Meg.

"I have none," said Hob. "It's all Hob can do to be brave. I think you should go. I do not like this. Go. Go."

"I can be brave too," said Meg. "I think."

"I shall look after her," said Tom.

The stone wall was the door to a different country. Hob and the two children were at the top of a slope, a forest falling away at their feet. They might have been in a hut high on a mountain, not in a cellar. There was a long vista to the sea. Clouds hung in the sky, and it was like a picture.

"Music," said Tom. They heard full and clear what had always been slow and far off, low and distant. A dancing tune romped along a path under the trees.

There was a man in a cloak. His back was hunched under some load, but the load did not stop him playing a violin. Among the trees, behind him, beside him, were other figures.

"Fluellen," said Hob. "Playing his way out."

"Why is it pretty?" asked Meg. "We do not like the children."

"Do not remember it," said Hob. "Fluellen has the crock of gold on his back, and the goblins are dancing so much they have not noticed. When he comes out the goblins will know what has happened, and come through."

"I don't see any king," said Tom. "Is that it walking?"

"Yes," said Hob. "Hob does not know what will happen. Nor does Fluellen; and the goblins are ignorant people."

Fluellen ought to have been old, but he was young and strong, carrying the crock and playing the fiddle without losing his breath. But the weight bowed his back.

He was looking back over his bent shoulder and smiling, smiling, with only a few paces to cover before reaching his own land, his own house, carrying victory, and endless wealth.

He turned to face the goblins. He ran his tune up to a triumphant end, tucked the fiddle under his arm, bowed mockingly, and was ready to step backward into safety.

Before he did so, something happened in the pretty forest. The trees moved and heaved and parted, and with crashing thunder began to fall to one side and another.

Hob stood smaller than Meg or Tom, little more than knee high to Fluellen or a Goblin. Now he drew in his breath, in and in, air hissing into his lungs. He grew to Meg's size, to Tom's, to Fluellen's, and bigger, tall and fierce, not the kindly though sharp-spoken Hob known to the children.

Out of the forest came what Hob had feared. It trod larger than an elephant, but on two legs. It had a head that was all jaw, and giant eyes. It had hands like claws. It walked like an earthquake, and the rock broke beneath it.

"As big as a house," said Hob. "I said so."

Fluellen should have stepped backward into the cellar sooner, and escaped with his stolen goods. But when he saw the goblin king he hesitated, and the moment was past.

As soon as the music stopped the goblins understood what was happening. They saw their crock of gold being taken by a mortal man, and came to prevent the theft.

"Get behind me, Fluellen," said Hob, in a mighty voice. "We deal with the goblins first, and then with their king." Hob thrust him to the back of the cellar. Fluellen fell down under the weight of the crock.

"There are three of us," said Hob. "To deal with goblins."

"So you shall," said Fluellen, picking himself up, and taking up the crock of gold again. "I don't know what you are, but I did not summon you."

"Stand and fight," Hob ordered. But Fluellen did not. He escaped up the stairs and into the house.

"Go Meg, go Tom," Hob roared. "I shall fight until the end."

Most of the goblins were without swords, because they had been dancing. But in moments they had them, and attacked the place where Hob stood. There was goblin blood, thick and black, and fallen goblins.

"I can't do it," said Meg. But she pushed her sword forward, and into something.

"Open your eyes," said Tom. "Goblins cut easily." Then he winced when he cut easily too, and there was red blood on a goblin blade. "It is nothing," he said.

The goblin king was advancing with his heavy

quick tread. Trees were scattered before him. The goblins ran forward, eager to please their king. Weight of numbers drove them past Hob and his helpers. Then some were coming back, because they had taken what they wanted. They had found Fluellen on the stairs, and were bringing him down.

He had been out of their country two minutes. In those two minutes he had changed from a young man to an old one, his hair white, his face lined. And he was calling for help. He was given a crust of goblin bread, which he ate ravenously.

Then, down the cellar steps came dwarfs with swords, and behind them Charlie with a sledgehammer.

EIGHTEEN

"It is my family in there,"
Alice had said very loudly, in the garden while three
dwarfs waved their swords about, but thought it
unwise to use them on her. "If people like you had
any family, which I doubt could be born to shrimps
with beards, you would know what I mean. So get
out of the way and let me get my family out.
Something is happening in that house and if you were
gentlemen instead of maggots that live in rotten trees
you would come to help me."

The dwarfs could tell that there would be trouble.
They lowered their swords and looked concerned.

"If you don't want your heads cracked," said
Charlie, picking up the sledgehammer, "you'll do
what she says, pretty quick. Come on, pass along the
car, and let the lady through."

The greenish light came fully into sight. Mrs. Idris
Evans, riding the broomstick, came upon the dwarfs

and the Grimeses suddenly, and had to jump off, so no one could prove she was a witch.

"It is dangerous to alight from a moving vehicle," said Charlie, who had seen that walk hundreds of times.

"Who are these little friends? " said Mrs. Idris Evans. "Curtsey to your auntie," she told the dwarfs. They looked very proud and ignored her. "Who are they, Mr. Grimes?"

"They are using real swords," said Charlie. "Look," and he showed her blood from his hip.

"Oh," said Mrs. Idris Evans, "this is to do with Fluellen. It'll be because you're here, that's all. I'll ask them what they are looking for." She used a sign language.

"They're looking for that Hob," she said. "But he's long gone. You wouldn't want him about, I can tell you."

"He's been away," said Alice, "but now he's in the house with the children."

Mrs. Idris Evans turned and calmly studied the house, the rocks turned to crystal and lit up, the noise that was walking round about it, the shaking of the ground.

"Goblins," she said. "There's been a breakout. I thought it was coming, with goblin children around. I've an idea that something worse than children will come out after them."

A mile away headlamps broke the sky at a crest of hill, and an engine began to race. Some vehicle was

coming at its best speed, faster than was healthy for
it, and keeping its speed up.

"It's in a hurry," said Charlie. "I know it sounds
like, but it can't be ..."

"Are you coming?" asked Mrs. Idris Evans.

"On my way," said Charlie.

"I'll wait outside," said Alice. "Charlie, get the
children out."

The dwarfs ran ahead. Charlie cantered after them,
swinging the sledgehammer. The dwarfs scented the
battle and were running down the cellar steps. Charlie
followed.

The cellar had only three walls now, because one
of them had opened up into a delightful landscape
where disagreeable things were happening.

Two ugly monsters were fighting. His own two
children were using swords and helping one of the
monsters.

"Come out of it, you two," Charlie bellowed.

"Come and help," called Meg. Charlie saw with
horror how she swung her sword with both hands
and neatly decapitated a grown-up goblin.

Charlie fought his way to the front. He sledged
goblins as he went, because they seemed to be the
enemy.

"Are you all right, mate?" he asked an elderly gen-
tleman with a mouth full of dry bread. He saw that
his face was like that of his own grandfather, in a
brown photograph he had had for years. "Fluellen?"
he asked. "Fluellen Grimes?"

The old man nodded his head.

"I'm your great-great-nephew," said Charlie. "We'll talk about this later. Get off you ruffian," he added to a wiry goblin that needed more than one sledging to lie down. "I must get my kids out. Your great-great-great-nephew and niece, but not brought up to fight."

Fluellen spat out a mouthful of crumbs. "I went down a young man, I spent an hour there, and came out ageing so fast that I knew I'd die before I got up the stairs, even if my housemaid Idris Evans has laid the tea by the fire. I've eaten goblin bread, and I'm going back in. Upstairs is too far."

With that he pushed past his great-great-grand-nephew Tom, ducked under the goblin king, and ran down the hill, striking wild notes on the violin.

Charlie was busy with goblins. He cleared them out from underfoot, and tripped on an earthenware pot. It jingled.

"He did it," said Charlie. "That's the crock of gold. That's what the goblins are after. That's family money, is that."

What he did then was guard Hob's back, without wanting to turn his back on Hob. Hob was seven feet tall and extremely strong. Beside him Meg and Tom were midgets, but fighting well. Tom was bleeding from two slashes on the arms.

In front of them were the three dwarfs, slicing like a delicatessen, skewering obstinate goblins, trimming off legs, and turning the side of the mountain into a butcher's shop.

Gradually the goblins began to despair. At last the dwarfs had nothing to fight. They looked at the goblin king, and thought better of fighting him. They looked at Hob, and thought the same again. They wiped their swords on their sleeves, scraped off black goblin blood, and made their way up the stairs and out of the cellar.

"Have we finished?" asked Charlie. "This is my cellar."

"I can't hold him," said Hob. "He is coming forward all the time. Swords are no good."

"I don't know who you are," said Charlie. "And I'm sure I don't want to. But Meg, and Tom, you come out of it at once."

"I'm just getting the hang of things," said Tom.

"I'm sick of them," said Meg.

Then Hob slipped on the black blood and went over on his back. At once the king moved forward, like some demon chess piece. Meg and Tom scrambled back, and Charlie pushed them up the stairs. Hob got himself up before he was trodden down by the king, and ran up after them. Charlie waited a moment to see whether he should put the sledge-hammer in.

The goblin king did not come into the cellar. It was obvious to it that the cellar steps were too small, so it took the proper route, which was upward, into the stone that was part of the cellar wall and part of the house wall upstairs, the standing stone that Charlie had mistaken for a door on the first night.

Behind it the stone turned dark again, and there
was only a cellar with chopped up goblins, and the
crock of gold.

Charlie picked up the crock and went upstairs.
Behind him the cellar lay quiet and small, unpleasant-
ly untidy, and smelling thick.

Charlie put the crock on the table and went to see
what was happening. There was a great deal of running about.

He thought the two men out there were policemen,
with peaked caps. Then he knew they were two
inspectors from his own depot in London. On the
road was his own bus, steam coming from its sides
after climbing the hills to Fairy Ring Cottage, its
indoor lamps on, standing as calm as if it were in
Battersea.

That was the only calm thing. Mrs. Idris Evans was
screeching in circles on her broomstick. Alice and the
children were running in several different directions.
The dwarfs were marching away. And Hob had
shrunk to his own size, shorter than his sword.

The goblin king was out on the surface now, turning about, waiting to see what there was to eat.

"We have failed," screeched Hob. "We have failed."

Inside the cottage Hob coming through the wall
seven feet high had addled Budgie's brain. "Fares
please," she was shouting. "Any more fares. Change
at the Elephant. This bus for Hounslow. Who's a good
boy, then. All aboard."

"Shut up," shouted Charlie. "Nup, nup, skwee! I've

had enough." But he heard some of the words Budgie was saying.

He ran outside. "Get in the bus," he called. "We're leaving."

"Oh, Charlie," said the inspector, not noticing any of the excitement, or thinking it was merely country life. This was the man who had sacked him a few weeks ago. "About that little business. We've had the same trouble all through the fleet, so we don't blame you anymore. It was mechanical failure, not your fault. We've come to get you back."

"I don't care," said Charlie. "Get in the bus. We're off."

"Someone's in it already," shouted the other inspector. "How dare they? Hey, you get out of that bus."

The headlamps of the bus came on. The engine began to run. The bus started to move. There was someone in the driving seat, wearing a driver's cap.

Hob sank to the ground beside Charlie. "I've done my best," he said. "The goblin king is loose, and I'm sorry."

The bus men were running to the bus. Alice and the children were behind the hedge. The witch had crashed into a snowman and bent her stick. Charlie and Hob were beside the cottage door, and the dwarfs long gone.

The goblin king circled the house, still looking for something to eat. It munched hedge, then spat it out. It took a chimney pot and mangled it. It ate a snowman's head. It roared.

Baby roared back. Búdgie made a sort of barking noise.

"Wants its neck wrung," said Charlie. "Our friend could do the job well."

NINETEEN

The goblin king, not in the least friendly, still paced in a quarrelsome way, biting the heads off trees. Lightning played round its head like a crown.

On the road, with all lights ablaze, horn on full, destination blinds whirring, and bell dinging, the red bus that Charlie had driven for seven years, had singled out its prey.

"Charlie," shrieked Alice, alarmed, sure Charlie must be driving into battle. The men who brought the bus from London stood in the snow, disappointed with the country, longing for a quiet traffic jam with angry taxi drivers.

"My old bus," said Charlie. "Not me. It's been hijacked."

Alice said nothing. She squeezed his hand.

But who was driving? "I wonder," said Hob.

The king and the bus sized each other up. The bus

blew a loud challenge at the king. The king honked back, shifted about, knocked down a garden wall, stamped its feet, climbed out of the resulting hole, and began to charge.

"Whoever you are," said Charlie, talking to his bus, "just take as much care as you can."

"Hob," said Meg. "Do something."

"What do you think I can do?" said Hob. "Set Budgie on it?" There was a shriek indoors, a thud, and the ghost of a skwee.

The bus made a bumpy trip right round the house, in and out of the tall standing stones.

The goblin king went round like a set of tanks. The bus kept its distance, flashing headlamps, or dinging its bell.

The king understood the rude remarks. It tiptoed round the other way. The bus slithered about in Fluellen's thorny hedges. Charlie heard paint being scratched off.

"It's where I lost my breeches," thought Hob.

A black thing came flying toward the king from the roadside, calling, "Excuse me, majesty, can I help you?"

"Whooff," went the goblin king, and blew away Mrs. Idris Evans, with a head-over-heels cat squalling. She and the cat landed in a snowdrift, waving black legs. The broomstick buried itself beside its mistress.

The driver backed the bus into the field next door, where the snow was untrodden. The driver put the lights out and waited, the great diesel engine chuckling.

The goblin king peered round a corner. The bus saw it, flashed a lamp, and uttered a tempting squeak or two with its bell. It roared its engine, defiantly. It was a brave bus, even if only the driver thought so.

"I ought to go and help," said Charlie. "That vehicle is too old to know what it's doing. It's my responsibility."

"And you are too young," said Hob, holding him down.

The bus chirruped. The goblin king replied in an uncharming way, like a belch.

Mrs. Idris Evans pulled herself out of the snow. She started up the broomstick, sat sidesaddle, and trailed her way down to the field. She was far smaller than the bus or the king, but blacker and more wicked. The broomstick was not running at all well, missing on several twigs.

The bus was almost silent now. Its engine still ran steadily, but there were no squeaks or lights or bells.

The goblin king floundered through the field, throwing up snow on either side, making a broad road with footprints in it. "Yah, yah?" it shouted menacingly. Are you there? it meant.

The bus said nothing. The king became excited about a rock. It started a conversation, shouted a conversation, didn't wait for a reply, wouldn't wait for a reply, and jumped on the rock. It kicked sand about, the remains of the rock.

The bus thought about that, and said even less than usual.

The goblin king picked a tree, as a child picks a primrose. It sharpened it with its teeth and waved it about.

The bus still said nothing. Its destination boards went pale, then black. But it gathered its courage and put up a defiant route number, 6.

"That's my girl," said Charlie. "I don't know what you are going to do, but I hope you succeed. It's a good number."

The king leaned on its tree and waited.

The engine of the bus made a jollier sound, a busy rumble. Its lights lit up again. It opened and closed its doors. Something in it gave a cheery shout, and it began to move.

"Go on, get in there," said Charlie. "Attack."

But the bus was not in attacking mood. It went away from the king, ignoring it. It stopped to let the black cat cross its path. The cat was pleased at this, thought it was giving mental orders and did it again, but the bus was out of patience, and did not stop. The cat dropped its impertinent swaggering tail and ran. It sat in the snow licking broken pride from its paws, did up its weskit buttons one by one with its tongue, then its trouser buttons, in the unprivate way cats have.

Mrs. Idris Evans, on the far side of the field, admired the goblin king from afar. Her mind ran through all the charms she knew, to see what could entice and overcome the creature.

The bus saw her as a passenger, stopped, opened

its door, and invited her aboard. A moment later she was on the top deck, choosing a front seat with care.

"The magic chair," Charlie breathed. "Not everyone knows."

The bus unhesitatingly plowed its way round the field, making a route past the king.

The king waited for battle. Hob waited for battle. But the bus had other ideas. It did what buses often do. It sailed past, taking no notice of trees being waved about, unaware of passengers.

"That's training," said Charlie. "He's a real busman."

The bus followed its old track right round again, like a toy train, and stopped. The king waved his tree, angry at not getting a fight started.

"Why doesn't he follow the bus?" asked Meg.

"The bus would get away," said Charlie. "It can do seventy miles an hour."

Mrs. Idris Evans got out. The bus was not taking her where she wanted to go. Then she had trouble starting her broomstick.

The bus started along its route again until it had turned the far corner. It growled all its gears.

"Winding up now," said Charlie. "There'll be a squabble."

The bus blew its hooter defiantly, rudely.

The king understood. It was used to the timetable now. It raised itself high, waving the tree, holding it in two great hands, ready to smite the bus as it passed.

The bus came on with a dark murk of torn-up

snow and diesel smoke following it.

"It won't do any good," said Charlie. "Just going round in circles forever. But that's the nature of buses."

The king stood ready, but the bus cheated. It was very simple. Instead of hurtling past, all bright lights and loud noises, it veered a little to one side, and did something buses ought not to do. It ran over a member of the public.

Ran over is perhaps what was intended. The unstoppable met the immovable, in fact. The bus went headfirst into the great goblinish mass. The king burst. The bus crumpled from front to back. Its lights went out, its hooter wailed. The destination blinds flipped to TERMINUS, and the engine died. Its last thuds faded with the last sighs of the goblin king.

"That center bearing," said Charlie. "I said it would go."

Out from the cab leaped the Gremlin, into the arms of Mrs. Idris Evans, who had come sputtering up on the broomstick, having to push it some of the way. "You don't want to bother with old ugly," said the Gremlin. "I saw you come a cropper on your run-about. I'll come home with you and fix it up, eh? I'm just as nasty in my quiet way."

"Honeychild," said Mrs. Idris Evans, leading him away.

"And I like your kiddies," said the Gremlin, hand in hand with Rag and Dew. "And your yummy kitten."

The goblin king fell to pieces in the snow. A crumpled bus squat as a tombstone stood beside the remains. There were no bones. Goblins are made of primitive stuff almost like water.

Alice took Baby indoors. The house was unharmed, but the fire was out. She lit it with the first things to hand, and put the kettle on it. Charlie asked about the crock of gold, which he had put on the table.

"Oh," said Alice, "those dead leaves? I lit the fire with them and filled the jar with ashes. I'm just making tea."

"That's what we want most," said Hob. "A bit of normal: family round the fire, Hob in the hearth, bird under a cloth to keep it quiet, and Baby gradually learning how to be one." Hob does not understand that Baby will change into a boy. "Family is family now," he thinks, "and that is how it should stay."

He yawned. Sleepy was tapping on his shoulder, "Tea first," said Hob. He yawned, putting his hand in front of his mouth to keep Sleepy out.

"Fire's getting noisy," said Charlie. Meg and Tom looked at him. They knew what the noise was. "I can know," said Charlie, "and still not believe. So there, Hob."

Charlie's unbelieving hand put a chocolate biscuit into a certain saucer, and the certain saucer inside the fender.

"Nup," said Budgie, teasingly.

"A piffle a glob," said Baby.